Praise for the
Private Invest

A Rainbow Murder
Mystery

"Fans of Travis McGee are in for a treat as Robert Downs' latest book, *Graceful Immortality*, delivers every bit of suspense, mystery, and femme fatales in bathing suits one expects from the genre McGee made famous. Casey Holden is a smart, smooth-talking PI who grabs the reader in a stranglehold and doesn't let go as the twists unfold. Murder might be first on his mind, but sex isn't far. So slather on the sunscreen, squeeze into those leg warmers, and prepare for a fun, wild mystery reminiscent of the late, great John MacDonald."

—J.A. Kazimer, author of *The Fairyland Murders*

"In his rollicking mystery *Graceful Immortality*, Robert Downs has created a wisecracking protagonist, Casey Holden, on par with Robert B. Parker's Spenser (though with perhaps an even more active libido). This fine mystery has suspects galore and more interesting women than even Casey can shake a stick at. *Graceful Immortality* is a well-written and fun-filled ride through the parlors and alleyways of Virginia Beach."

—D.E. Johnson, author of *Detroit Shuffle*

"Think of Mike Hammer. Then think of James Bond (as portrayed in the films, not the one in the books). Merge them into a single character and you have Casey Holden, PI. Add a plot that could have come from the pen of Mickey Spillane. A cold case, sexy women, and dialog that races along like Holden's Viper—fast, flashy, and eye-popping. *Falling Immortality* is, for fans of macho, slick talking, wise cracking sleuths, a must read."

—Frederick Ramsay, author of the Ike Schwartz mysteries

"Meet Casey Holden, former cop, now a PI facing the most dangerous combination that can confront a shamus: a beautiful woman with secrets and hard men who don't want him to find them. Like a post-modern Mike Hammer, Holden doesn't lack self-confidence or the quick comeback—or the tendency to find trouble. Robert Downs' debut novel, *Falling Immortality*, skillfully tips its fedora at the hard-boiled mystery genre. It's fast-paced, tightly structured and keeps you guessing until the end. This will be a writer and series to watch."

—Jon Talton, author of the David Mapstone Mysteries
and the Cincinnati Casebooks

continued

"Rob Downs has created the classic, basically 'good man', in a sometimes very wicked world. An original, very vivid journey through society's weakness and perversity. Casey Holden is an excellent Virgil to this modern underworld. The characters are fully fleshed, the dialogue sharp and racy. *Falling Immortality* is a superb read. A real enjoyment."
—Paul Doherty, author of the Hugh Corbett Medieval Mystery series and The Sorrowful Mysteries of Brother Athelstan series

"A ribald joyride with a wise-cracking PI and a bevy of babes!"
—Gerald Elias, author of *Danse Macabre* (2010, St. Martin's Press)

"*Falling Immortality* by Robert Downs is a wild ride from the first page to the last. Casey Holden is the quintessential gumshoe, both fearless and foolish. In this debut novel, Downs has created a character with tremendous potential to grow and evolve. Equally compelling is Det. Ian Jackard, Holden's former partner and reluctant inside man at the Virginia Beach PD. Bottom line: this series is sure to be a worthy addition to the genre. This novel has truly earned a 5/5 rating."
—Jud Hanson, BestSellersWorld.com

"*Falling Immortality* is, rather, all about character, in particular that of series lead Casey Holden. He's good looking and witty, with an abundance of money and sex appeal to back him up. And he's the first to say so. The women in his life, his new client notwithstanding, aren't wallflowers or pushovers, but when up against the Holden charm offensive they don't stand a chance. The bottom line here is, to enjoy this book you have to buy into the character."
—Hidden Staircase Mystery Books

"The book itself is well put together in short, easy-to-read chapters with adequate editing, an eye-catching cover, and a tantalizing sneak preview of the author's next book in the back. I look forward to reading subsequent novels in the series as this first-time author continues to develop his characterization and writing style."
—Reading New Mexico

Graceful Immortality

Casey Holden, Private Investigator

Robert Downs

ROBERT DOWNS

Rainbow Books, Inc.
FLORIDA

Library of Congress Cataloging-In-Publication Data

Downs, Robert, 1980-
  Graceful immortality : Casey Holden, private investigator / Robert Downs. – First edition.
    1 online resource. – (Casey Holden, private investigator ; 2)
  Description based on print version record and CIP data provided by publisher; resource not viewed.
    ISBN 978-1-56825-170-7 (softcover : acid-free paper) – ISBN 978-1-56825-171-4 (epub ebook)
  1. Private investigators–Fiction. 2. Murder–Investigation–Fiction. I. Title.
  PS3604.O9526
  813'.6–dc23

2014036584

Graceful Immortality: Casey Holden, Private Investigator
Copyright © 2014 by Robert Downs

RobertDowns.net

Softcover ISBN: 978-1-56825-170-7
EPUB ISBN: 978-1-56825-171-4

Published by
Rainbow Books, Inc.
P. O. Box 430
Highland City, FL 33846-0430

Editorial Offices and Wholesale/Distributor Orders
Telephone (863) 648-4420
Facsimile (863) 647-5951
RBIbooks@aol.com
RainbowBooksInc.com

Individuals' Online Orders
Amazon.com • www.AllBookStores.com

The paper used in this publication meets the minimum requirements of the American National Standard for Information Sciences–Permanence of Paper for Printed Library Materials, ANSI Z39.48-1984.

First edition 2014
18 17 16 15 14   5 4 3 2 1
Produced and Printed in the United States of America.

For Jen—
you make my heart dance

Other books by Robert Downs—

Falling Immortality: Casey Holden, Private Investigator (Rainbow
Books, Inc., 2011)

Graceful Immortality

1

Kathryn Gable had come into my office with a stern look on her face, her chin held high, wearing a dress of fussy green. She had introduced herself, sat down in the chair before my desk and said, "I understand you have a reputation."

In my previous life, I was a cop with little respect for authority or the chain of command for the Virginia Beach PD. Looking back on the situation now, I had lasted five years, three years longer than I would've assumed possible. As a private investigator, I'm allowed to have no respect for authority, no filter for my mouth or my brain, determine my caseload, and take vacations when the mood strikes me . . . In fact, I'd just returned from one of those vacations the day before Kathryn had arrived in my office.

I smiled at Kathryn and wondered what she'd heard, though I wasn't quite ready to go back to work again. My response was somewhat indifferent as I managed, "Oh, really?"

"Word travels," she said.

"In what way? Tell me about it."

"You're good at what you do."

I took that as a compliment, leaned back in my leather chair and waited for her to continue. She paused as she gathered her thoughts, and I waited.

Maybe my dad wouldn't roll over in his grave at my mere existence. As for my mom, she'd always been proud of me no matter what I did. I could have been a coal miner for all she cared. And I had their trust fund to keep me afloat—the one thing they hadn't done when their luxury yacht went down in a storm off the Mexican coast. Their money backed me up during rough times, unscrupulous clients, vacations . . .

Kathryn crossed her legs, dainty-like, then she uncrossed them again. The dress showed off her legs to perfection. I enjoyed the sight of an attractive woman. And those legs meant she took good care of herself—she liked to run, dance, or swim. I voted for swimming.

"Well, are you willing to help me?"

The ball was in my court, and I had my smashing forehand ready to go. "That depends on what I'm going to help you do." Hiring me was serious and, in some cases, funny business, and I guessed this was what she had in mind. The serious aspect, not the funny one.

"Here's the deal," she said. "I'm a dancer, and one of my associates has been murdered. It's a delicate situation. I'm told you're the man for the job."

Murdered? I took a deep breath and let my thoughts drift back to my previous case, involving one crazy wife, a crooked cop, a neglectful ME, two henchmen the size of linebackers, a fall from the roof of The Hot Spot, and a very sore hand. Trouble always managed to find me.

That's how it had been with my parents, too. First it had been a near miss in their private jet, a belly landing when the gear wouldn't lower, but in that case the pilot had saved the day with an ace's high, full-stall landing. Then it had been an Italian sports car off a narrow road in the Swiss Alps, which carried them into a deep ravine. Just one thing after another—they'd walked away laughing, and then the damn storm at sea had caught up with them. I tried not to think about those fantastic people who'd been my parents, but I just couldn't help it.

"Well?" Kathryn said.

I came up for air. Oh, yes, murder. "Why don't you just relax and tell me all about—the murder. Then I'll make a decision on whether or not I can help you. Okay?"

"I'm talking about Jessica Mason—she was found dead in the parking lot of the Virginia Dance Company."

She stared at me with wide amber eyes, not a tear in sight. I made a mental note of that and asked, "How long has she been dead?"

"Two days." Kathryn crossed her legs and sighed, as if suddenly all of this were too much for her. "We've been trying to reach you for the past two days. You should work on making yourself more available to clients. For one who comes so well recommended, you need a secretary or an assistant."

I laughed. "My obligations allow me breaks now and then, and I take full advantage of them. How come you didn't find someone else to help you? Why me?"

I was puzzled still and even feeling trapped. The confines of my office were closing in on me: two client chairs, a window, my leather chair, a single filing cabinet, my fine mahogany desk, a computer, a coffee maker, and no vacations ahead.

Kathryn said, "I've been told it's not in our best interest to hound the police. We want someone more discreet, and you're about as discreet as they come. We don't want to create a big scene involving the local authorities in any way."

"Okay. But I'll need to see the body." I couldn't help myself. I didn't mean her body with the gorgeous legs, thigh tapping, and fussy dress. I could focus on the matter at hand when necessary. I straightened in my cozy chair and tried to look official.

Kathryn's amber eyes stared at me, as if I might've misplaced my mind. "What for?" she demanded.

"An autopsy."

She jumped, startled. "You're going to conduct it yourself?"

I held up my hand. "No. But someone will have to do it. I still have contacts from my former cop life; those contacts place me in a good position to ask questions, get favors, bargain."

"But an autopsy?"

"To figure out exactly what happened. Dead bodies have stories to tell, and I need to know her story. She might sing like a canary, and we won't even know it until an autopsy is performed. I presume that's being done now or in the near future."

"I really don't understand. She's dead. What more does anyone need to know?"

"Lots," I said. "A reason for her death comes in handy. First and foremost, if there is no obvious cause of death, an autopsy is mandatory. That's the law. Also, if we can figure out why, then we can probably figure out who. Those two questions often go together. Where is the Virginia Dance Company located?"

"Norfolk. Jessica's body was found splayed on the pavement at the far end of our parking lot—away from the overhead lights."

I leaned back and considered the situation. After the pause, I said, "I'm thinking someone didn't want her found right away."

"One could make that assumption," she said.

"What would you assume?"

"That her killer wanted her to be found by a specific person. Jessica was a well-known, well-liked member of the VDC, even though she was a private person."

I straightened in my chair and leaned forward against my desk, thinking.

"Are dancers ever stalked, threatened?" I asked.

"More often than you might think. We've been known to have crazy fans."

It was getting interesting. I relaxed and allowed Kathryn

Gable to hire me, after several more questions and answers, plus general conversation during which she came close to begging. Almost begging sealed the deal for me.

She opened her purse, pulled out a checkbook, and wrote me a check for my retainer.

I stood up, accepted the check, thanked her, and promised to be in touch.

Kathryn nodded and left my office, those gorgeous, long legs in high heels taking her where she wanted to go.

And now Jessica Mason's dead body entered my life in all of her infinite glory.

I took a deep breath, made myself a cup of coffee, and returned to my desk to sit in my leather chair and stare out my window, which faced the brick wall of another building. It wasn't a scene to enjoy, but it was a place to think.

I thought about making a call I hadn't made in several years—to Isabel Titler, the medical examiner who by now had done, or was about to do, Jessica's autopsy. Well, maybe. She had to share the stage with another ME in her department.

Isabel and I had been an item, a serious item, and I wondered how her voice would sound and other stuff I didn't want to remember. Still, there was no other way to get the inside scoop on Jessica's demise without talking with Isabel before they sent Jessica off to the crematorium, followed by a memorial service.

But first, while I determined my angle before that phone call, I turned to the computer and asked it to tell me what it knew about Jessica Mason and the Virginia Dance Company of Norfolk.

2

For two hours I searched the Internet, drank black coffee with two sugars, and paused from time to time to stare out my window and rock back and forth in my leather chair. Without too much trouble I immersed myself in the world of dance.

For instance, I learned Virginia had only two professional dance companies. The Virginia Dance Company was the larger of the two organizations with fourteen principal dancers—now thirteen with Jessica Mason dead.

Dancers appeared to be chosen from modern, jazz, tap, character, and ballet. Most professional dancers started dancing before kindergarten, and I assumed most of the male dancers were gay. Dancing, it seemed, was first and foremost a business—and a cutthroat one at that. Modern dance originated in Europe around 1900, as if I cared. But there it was. I made a note of it; one never knew what might help along the way.

At last I pulled myself together and punched in that number on my cell phone I hadn't called in ages.

Isabel answered the phone with a crisp, "Medical examiner's office."

I took a deep breath and managed, "Hi, Isabel."

She recognized my voice. "What do you want?" Her voice was

quiet, careful, as if I might be some kind of explosive device that one had to handle with extreme care.

I appreciated the compliment and said, "I need to ask you a favor." I tried to keep it on the upbeat and easy, as if nothing had gone wrong between us.

"Oh?" she said.

"I'd like for you to check on a body for me . . . " Suddenly I realized I had high hopes for a new beginning, middle, and end with Isabel. She had a body with curves in all the right places.

Our relationship began with a few drinks, a few laughs, a few rolls in the hay, and then we parted ways, not once, but twice. I told myself it was nothing special, or so I thought. I needed to climb higher mountains and surf across choppier waters. I wondered now if I'd been wrong. Isabel was something to think about.

"You working a case?" she asked.

"Yes, and they're planning the memorial service as we speak." I didn't know that for sure, but it might help me get Isabel to ignore the past and think of the future, perhaps with the two of us together again . . .

"This is not a safe place to live, and I'm busy." She might have been talking to a child. "And I really don't have time for this."

"Please . . . for the good times?"

She sighed, as if relenting. "I recall a vacation with sandy beaches, soft beds, and two frisky people. But those days are long gone. You walked out on me."

I didn't deny it. She had mentioned marriage. And I didn't want to go there. Staying free was the name of the game, as far as I was concerned.

Perhaps I wasn't too smart. Isabel was the smartest of all, and the smart ones managed to get me in trouble. They left my tongue tied in knots, and they never forgave me, no matter what. The smart ones ruled the world, and the rest of us did our best to keep up.

Isabel interrupted my reverie. "Well, I'm hanging up. I've had enough of this—"

"Don't," I said. "I do need your help."

"Look. You walked away from me—twice. Nobody gets a third chance. Understand? Nobody."

"We'll see about that," I said.

I helped myself to as many women as possible. I liked at least one blonde at all times, and Isabel was as blond and beautiful as they came. How she had beat back the guys enough to make it through medical school, plus all the additional education required to become a medical examiner, defied understanding. I don't know why she hadn't ended up in jail along the way, not because of the guys, but just because she was Isabel.

I took a sip of my coffee, and the memories came crawling back. I smiled as I recalled how she got picked up for sunbathing nude on a public beach and how I, Casey Holden, then a cop, helped her beat the rap in court and saved her from a hefty fine. Oh, yes, she showed me her wild side during our brief time together. Lots of sex, not to mention a broken bed frame. That didn't scare me, but her wild side did.

"Truce," I said. "We shouldn't talk about the past. I was wrong. Let's keep it present tense. I need to know how Jessica Mason died. Have you done her autopsy?"

"Howard—he could've done it. I told you we're busy. I told you this town is not a nice place to live these days. Whoever screams the loudest for their need-to-know gets my attention. That's how it works"

"Well, would you check on Jessica Mason for me? I'd appreciate it."

"Keep in touch," she said.

And the line went dead.

Well, she did say, "Keep in touch."

I'd do just that tomorrow . . . But first I'd go around and see what Jessica's parents had to say about their daughter. That might prove interesting. They could tell me something about Jessica Mason I needed to know.

3

Tomorrow attacked me like a virgin.

I crawled out of bed, dropped to the floor of my apartment, and did five hundred push-ups and sit-ups. Then I took a shower and prepared for the day.

I slipped on a pair of jeans, a light blue t-shirt, and slid into a pair of brown Cole Haan loafers. Then I checked myself out in the mirror on the back of my closet door—looking good. Blond hair gelled, face shaved smooth, teeth sparkling, hazel eyes alert. I was ready for the day.

I had my 2005 Dodge Viper SRT-10, and I was out of excuses. I bypassed my office with the mahogany desk and black leather chair, having memorized the names and the address Kathryn Gable had given me for Jessica Mason's parents.

With my office in Norfolk, I know my way around. It wasn't long until I was parking my Viper in front of 2299 Overbrook.

Frank and Jill Mason lived on a shady street in a ranch style red brick house with white shutters over the windows. Out front was a flag pole with the stars and stripes at half-mast.

Perhaps in honor of Jessica's demise.

I rang the doorbell.

A man opened the door and said, "We're not talking to strangers. Keep it brief."

I introduced myself. "I'm here about your daughter. May I come in?"

He opened the door; I slipped into what proved to be the living room; he closed the door behind me. A petite woman stood to one side.

"What about our daughter?" I gathered he was Frank.

I flashed my PI license. "I presume the police have been in touch with you?"

"Two days ago," he said.

The lay of the land wasn't encouraging. Plastic covered the living room furniture. Knickknacks cluttered shelves on either side of a fireplace. The carpet was at least ten years old. What's more, imitation artwork filled part of the available wall space. It needed help, except for the rest of the walls, which were taken up by photographs of Jessica.

Most of the photographs involved Jessica dancing at various stages of her life. Several of the more recent photos showed off her raven hair to perfection. She had been attractive and then some. The décor transplanted the 1950s to the present, and there was enough Lysol in the air to cause a sinus infection.

One minute their daughter exemplified the room; the next minute she didn't. Her photos transported me back in time. I tried not to account for the differences.

I pulled myself together and said, "I was hoping you might talk with me. I've been hired by your daughter's employer to find out information regarding her death."

"So you're the one who's supposed to solve the crime," Frank said. "I hope you're smarter than the two cops we already spoke to. I wouldn't trust either one of them to find my cat."

"You don't have a cat." None of the telltale signs assaulted my senses.

"See?" Frank turned to his wife, "He's already smarter than the two nitwits from before." Then he turned back to me. "You should have a seat. If you stand any longer you're going to make me nervous."

I sat down on the plastic covered sofa. Then I waited for the Masons to sit as well.

In time Frank dropped into a plastic covered lounge chair, and Jill sat down on the very edge of a plastic covered straight back chair. Having settled in, they stared at me, as if waiting for me to do something, anything. Their faces carried nothing but expectation.

"I'd like to ask you a few questions about Jessica."

"What do you want to know?" Jill asked. Her voice was soft, compact, filled with hurt.

"I'm a detail person," I said. "Often the slightest piece of information helps me solve a case. I have a ball of thread in my hand, and I need to start unraveling it. Right now I don't even know how big the ball is. So, just tell me anything you want to share about your daughter."

"Just how detailed?" Jill asked.

"For instance, would anyone have wanted Jessica dead?"

"Not that we know of. Let me just tell you about her. And maybe that will help."

I spread my hands in open invitation, all part of the listening act. "Let's talk about Jessica."

Her face lit up. "Thank you," she said. She swallowed. "Jess was studious. She focused on dance, always had some cause she was chasing, whether it was sick animals or sick people. She was quite a performer, loved the stage, very expressive, emotional, talented. She couldn't watch a sad movie without a box of tissues beside her, and she'd go through every last one of them. She could dance her way into anyone's heart. I just can't believe she's gone. I refuse to believe she's gone . . . "

I waited while Jill collected herself.

Frank cleared his throat. "Is that enough for you?"

"Did you identify the body?" I asked.

"I didn't want her to go." He thumbed at his wife. "She wouldn't let me go without her. It was awful. There she was, dead, like she was ready for the butcher." Frank shook his head.

"I have a few more questions," I said.

"If it will help you," Jill said.

"How long had Jessica been with the VDC?"

"Almost two years."

I said, "Long enough to make a few enemies?"

"Or a few friends."

"I gather from the photos in the room she's been involved with dance most of her life," I said.

Jill glowed as she described her daughter. "In one form or another. Jess had dreams of opening her own studio. She was dedicated, always focused. She'd been teaching dance since college. She liked to help people. It drove her. She was a giver, not a taker."

"Did you see her perform often?"

"Oh, yes," Jill said. "Every chance we got. It's important to support your child in whatever they do. Do you have children?"

"No, I'm not married." I closed off the discussion before more questions ensued. "Any admirers in the crowd?"

"She always had admirers. She was very selective about who she chose to spend time with. She'd had a few boyfriends, a few girlfriends, nothing much beyond that." She paused. "Why would someone want to kill her?"

"That's what I plan to find out."

Frank returned to the conversation now, asking, "You working with the police?"

"I try to work with them as little as possible. I'm a former cop, the key emphasis being on the word former. I don't regret my cop days. I just have a different way of doing things." I didn't add: "Holden showed a lack of respect for authority and a strong, independent nature." That's how my evaluation had read.

"More of a loner, huh?"

"You could say that. A cowboy minus the saddle."

"Hope you have the proper horse," he said.

"I have all the horses I need."

This pointless conversation went on for another thirty minutes or so, repeating itself. All I learned was how painful it was to have a daughter die and not know why.

I drove to my office no wiser than I had been yesterday.

4

My cell phone rang while I drove away from the Mason's house.

I answered, "Holden here."

"Just what the heck do you think you're doing?" It was my VBPD cop friend, Detective Ian Jackard.

I had the steering wheel in one hand and my cell phone in the other. It wasn't the safest way to drive a muscle car, but it could have been worse.

"I'm investigating a murder," I said.

"Why is Dr. Titler nosing around the morgue for you?"

"What did she say about me?"

"You don't want to know. Nothing nice, buddy."

I tried not to groan. No use in letting anyone know I cared. Otherwise, I might have a list of admirers as long as a Phish concert.

Ian rushed on, saying, "You didn't answer my question. Why is your former lady love nosing around the morgue on your behalf?"

He had spoken slowly, as if I might be new to the English language. There were days I might have been willing to agree with him.

"Because she works there?"

"Don't act funny with me, Casey. Out with it."

"Because I asked her to find out about Jessica Mason's autopsy. How's that?"

"Howard Brien already performed one."

"And we know what a great job he did the last time."

On my previous case Howard had somehow messed with the investigation. I just couldn't prove it. And there was more I didn't like about him. He had a high-pitched voice, a habit of denying my requests, and a sarcastic nature. He also may or may not have attempted to obstruct justice. Once again, I just couldn't prove it.

"Don't you know how to leave things alone?" Ian asked.

"No. I'm paid to find answers."

"If there's a delay in the cremation, you're going to be the one to notify the family. Either that body is cremated today or your name is mud."

"What's the rush? It's not like she's going anywhere. What did the autopsy say?"

Click.

At the next traffic light, I flicked the steering wheel with my left hand. Everybody was hanging up on me.

I tossed my cell phone on the passenger seat and kept my foot on the gas. I wasn't treating Ian's call lightly. But if they sent Jessica off to be cremated today, well, okay. That wouldn't change the lab report, and Isabel could always tell me at her convenience.

Since the murder scene was on my list of places to visit, I decided to go there next and give Isabel a chance to get her house in order.

I drove to the almost empty parking lot of the Virginia Dance Company. I found a parking slot near the rather large building, removed myself from my Viper, locked it, and looked around.

Lots of lighting was evident near the building. But farther out, and on the fringes of the lot, no lights existed. So much for that. I tucked the layout in my mental folder for future reference, then

I turned to the building. It had double doors, and when I pushed on one, it opened for me. I stepped inside.

Before I knew what was happening, a girl was in front of me, smiling. She wore a short pink skirt and pink tights. Her head bounced, and so did she, before she rocked backward on her heels.

"What are you doing here?" she asked.

"Is this where the party is?"

I glanced around at the reception area. It could've used a makeover—six chairs covered in fake leather, a Degas print on the far wall, and an odor that spoke of bleach. The floor was covered in ceramic tiles with dancers in various dance positions engraved at random intervals. I assumed it all made sense. But not to me.

"Party?" the girl said. "Are you some kind of smartass?"

"That's me," I said. I gave her one of my best grins. It didn't work, and I was pretty sure it wasn't me. "I'm a smartass extraordinaire."

"Who are you?" she asked. Her hair was in pigtails, and she didn't look a day over sixteen. However, her attitude told a different story.

I followed my instincts. "Casey Holden," I said. "I'm a private eye."

"Or a private investigator?"

"Yeah, I do that too. But only on Sundays."

"What else do you do?"

"I make jokes. I'm full of them. I have a good one about a pirate, a parrot, and a steering wheel—"

She turned her nose up. "I've heard that one, and it's not very nice. Now, tell me, what kind of PI are you?"

"The kind that catches the bad people." Then I added, "By the way, who are you?" She'd been so busy pounding me into the ground it was time I learned about my opponent.

"My name, you mean?"

"That would be a good place to start."

"Lana Ralstein." She didn't offer her hand, and I didn't offer mine. "I'm a dancer."

And without further ado, guess who appeared before us?

Yes, that's right. Kathryn Gable. She popped out of the wine bottle like a cork headed straight for the moon. Or, in this case, a door just off the main entryway.

I was prepared to have a cordial, civilized conversation with Kathryn. There was no avoiding her. I dug in my heels, smiled, and was about to speak when Kathryn beat me to it.

"So, what are you doing here?" she asked.

"I'm here to make sure people like you two stay out of trouble."

Lana's sober face broke into laughter. Once the laughter ceased, she said, "That's going to be a full-time job."

"I've got all the time in the world," I said.

"You have more time than I do," Kathryn said.

I assumed that last jab of Kathryn's denoted her imminent departure. Not so. She stayed on.

Lana said, "Are you here to just observe or what?" Her question was just innocent enough to make her look as cute as a schoolgirl with those pigtails.

"You never know," I said. "Something interesting may happen, and it just might be what I need to know." If I had been a fire marshal I was sure I could've discovered a code violation.

"Or you might be here just to cause problems," Kathryn said. "I've been thinking about that t-shirt you were wearing yesterday with the saying on it that mentioned swingers. I should've taken a hint from that. Based on your current attire, though, you decided to one-up yourself."

"I've been known to out-duel even the fiercest of competitors," I said.

Yesterday Kathryn had been my friend—well, I thought so. Yesterday Kathryn had begged me to work for the VDC. Today the cornsilk stare-down had ensued. It was as if she'd changed her mind about me and wanted to drive me crazy.

Kathryn exhaled a sigh of resignation. "Once you're in, you're in. For better or worse, in sickness and in health, 'til death do us part. In other words, we're stuck with you. Is that your moral code?"

I stared at her. What was the matter with this woman? I was as close to the James Bond type as a woman would ever get. I figured I did them a service by just showing up. But it all boiled down to a t-shirt with the innocent saying, SWINGERS TENNIS TOURNAMENT. I didn't even play tennis, and I didn't figure anybody could argue with that.

Before I had a chance to defend the t-shirt, Kathryn rushed on to say, "Some of us have work to do. Not all of us have the privilege of taking up space for a living. I'm surprised you can do your job with a straight face."

I'd had enough. "Look. I'm as straight as they come. They don't make arrows as straight as I am. And I'm the best at what I do. You can ask anyone, preferably women." I smirked. "I'm a man focused on the thrill of the chase, success, and making up my own rules." It even said as much in my last performance review, and nearly all the previous ones, when I was a cop.

"According to whom?" Kathryn demanded.

I stepped over to Lana, placed my hand on her shoulder, and smiled.

She smiled right back and said, "As my father used to say, 'Why send a telegram if you have the t-shirt?' "

Kathryn was not impressed. She looked like she was ready to bolt. I had a feeling she always looked that way around men. It wasn't worth the effort to ask her to sing soprano. I had other matters to attend to.

"How hard is your job?" Lana asked. "I bet it's harder than Kathryn thinks. I'll stick to dancing. It's what I've always been good at. Do you know how much strength it takes to go on pointe? All football players should be required to take ballet."

Yeah, like that would ever happen. Discovering a virus to take down Apple would prove easier.

"It takes more work than just standing around looking cute," I said. "Being a PI is more frustrating than fun, but it does have its benefits." I paused and upped an eyebrow. "Of course, I do have a lot to learn about the whole ballet thing."

"And the benefits would be?" Lana was loving our conversation.

"I'm still trying to work through them all, but when I get some answers, I'll let you know," I said. "I'm sure you're concerned."

Kathryn harrumphed. "I still don't know why you're here."

"I'm investigating a murder. When somebody gets whacked, I want to find out what's going on. What better place to learn and observe than the very place that employed Jessica Mason?" I was at my best when I stirred up trouble. I was fairly certain I had a t-shirt in my collection that mentioned as much.

Kathryn said, "That's good to know." Then she vanished faster than I could summon a genie in a bikini.

I was pretty sure I hadn't imagined her.

"So, how long are you going to be around?" Lana asked.

"As long as it takes."

"To what?"

"To figure out what's going on here."

"In that case," she said, "let me show you around."

5

Lana Ralstein gave me the fifty cent tour of the dance studio. I saw three large rehearsal spaces, a couple of offices—one was filled with several cubicles, and the other wasn't—several women in tights and a couple of men, some dancing and some jiggling. The main corridor had three additional Degas prints, all fake, of course. The end of the main corridor formed a T with the rehearsal spaces on one side and the offices on the other, and all three rehearsal spaces were covered in cherry hardwood. Soft rock played in one of the rehearsal rooms, jazz played in the other, and the third room was vacant.

After the less-than-ten-minute tour, Lana told me she had to get ready for a rehearsal, and I asked if I could watch. She told me to get a life, and then she was gone.

I was left to my own devices, so I decided to take up space in the largest rehearsal room, with the soft rock and a large number of women, and watch the events as they unfolded. I voted for more dancing, especially the naked kind.

I didn't get to visit the dressing rooms—where all the action took place. If I had gotten to see a striptease or two I probably would have had a much more favorable opinion of the Virginia Dance Company's facilities. Instead I'd have to make do with the images my mind could conjure up. I had one or two good ones, and I was working on a third when one of the male dancers crossed paths with me. My first impression was that he was gay.

"Who are you?" I asked.

He echoed me.

"I asked you first."

"I'm a principal dancer with the VDC. Bradley Cassidy."

I told him my name, and I stuck out my hand.

He didn't take it.

I said, "What kind of a name is Bradley Cassidy?"

There is no way he's straight.

"It's the name I was given at birth."

I didn't like his smirk, the way he looked over my head when he spoke, or the way he had turned up his nose at my hand.

"Can you change it?"

"Why would I want to do a thing like that?" he asked. He had to look up at me, he was so short, and he was as skinny as a tree branch.

"I don't know," I said. "It's just a thought."

"Well, you can keep your thoughts to yourself."

I wanted to make a comment about his tights and how I was surprised that he was even able to speak in a normal tone of voice, but I couldn't think of a way not to offend him. Since I wasn't in an offending mood, I decided to let it pass.

"I'm not sure I can do that," I said.

"Well, then you might find yourself getting your butt kicked." He stood a little taller, and then he placed his fist in the palm of his other hand.

I had my back against the wall. He and I were the only ones away from the door, the others had congregated on the other side of the room. I took a step forward to let him know who was boss. I could hear voices down the hall—they weren't coming our way. I smiled; he didn't. He looked at me out of the corner of his eye, and then he focused on another dancer at the other end of the hall. The moment of silence lingered, and I wasn't sure I wanted it to end.

He started to walk away. I decided to take advantage of the situation before the opportunity was lost forever. "What do you know about Jessica Mason?"

"I wasn't aware we were playing twenty questions." He wiped a strand of red hair out of his eyes.

"If you keep up the attitude—"

"I don't do well with threats," he said. "If it's information you seek, you're going about it the wrong way."

"You're going to be playing a lot more than twenty questions. I just might take you outside and kick your scrawny ass. You couldn't weigh more than one-forty, and that's sopping wet."

"I'd like to see you try."

"I wouldn't need to try." I don't like guys smaller than me telling me what I can and can't do. I didn't like mouthy little rascals, either.

"Now we've resorted to threats," Bradley said.

"We didn't resort to anything," I said. "I'm not sure I like your attitude enough to believe your story.

"I haven't told you my story."

"And I'm not sure I want to hear it," I said. I still needed to decide where Bradley Cassidy stood on a lot of matters, and the best way to find out a few things was to stir up the competition. As far as I was concerned, it was all competition.

"What's your deal?" he asked.

"What's yours? You're awfully confrontational for a man who's half my size." It was a slight exaggeration.

"Do you have any idea what dancing does to a guy? I'm on my feet all day long. I've had black toes and blue ones, broken toes, stubbed and skinned ones, thigh cramps, twisted knees, turned ankles—"

"Turns him into a fairy," I said.

He wasn't amused by my comment. "Not hardly. There's a lot more to it than that. Dancing is more macho than football and basketball combined. It's as hard on your feet as running, and I don't have the benefit of padded shoes and cushioned socks."

"You're one strange dude," I said.

"It's a competition."

"Life?"

"Dancing," he said. Bradley looked at me like I didn't have a clue.

He was right on target. And I wasn't even sure I could learn. There weren't enough hours in the day to teach me everything I needed to know about dancing. In spite of that, I decided to start with the basics and work up from there. Maybe I'd get lucky. "I thought it was an art form."

"It's that, too," Bradley said. "But it's a lot more of a struggle than you'd imagine. And when you least expect it, it will suck you right in. When that spotlight hits me, my whole world lights up, and I forget about all the crap going on in my life."

I changed tactics. "How well did you know Jessica?"

"I knew her as well as anybody. Probably better than most. We were lovers."

"You're pretty open about it," I said.

"I have nothing to hide. Despite your best efforts to tell me otherwise."

"Usually those who say their life is an open book are just putting up a front," I said. "They're busy steering you in another direction. You can try to do that with me, but you won't get very far. I know what I'm doing." Or I hoped I did. When you started at the bottom, it was a long, bumpy ride to the top.

"Thanks for the tip. I'll be sure to keep that in mind when I'm banging your girlfriend."

"How did you know I have a girlfriend?" I had two, in fact, but I wouldn't tell Bradley that. He might use his newfound knowledge against me. In an investigation, it was important to always have the upper hand.

"When you're around girls long enough, it's pretty easy to tell the guys who do and the guys who don't. You're not one to be without. In fact, you've probably got them lined up and ready to go."

"What the heck are you talking about?" I said.

"Girls bring guys into the mix," Bradley said, "and I keep my eyes open. I may not be in the best profession, in your opinion, but I know what I'm doing. I watch things, notice others, and I pick up more than most."

I hoped I did the same. "I'm not sure I ever know what I'm doing. It's touch and go every step of the way."

"Then how did you get where you are? By accident?"

"I open enough cans and something's bound to pop out. So, tell me more about Jessica. You're one of my best links to her past. You got a better view than most."

"She was just your typical girl. We had fun together."

And you're just the typical guy.

"I'm sure you did. What was her personality?"

"She was emotional, quick tempered, cried as often as she frowned, had a few close friends, no real enemies—"

"So why did she end up dead?"

"Your guess is as good as mine," he said.

"See, that's the problem; I don't want to guess."

6

"Just how crazy are you?" Bradley Cassidy asked.

I'd lost track of how many times I'd heard that question. "If you ever figure out the answer, I'd like to know. I've had a few people ask me, and I've never been able to give them a straight answer."

He'd had enough, I guess. With that he gave me a long, hard look, a cocky salute of sorts, and went into the hall to disappear from view.

I heard music from somewhere else in the building, accompanied by a bunch of thumping, as if people might be flying all over the place and running into walls. I guessed some kind of rehearsal.

Enough was enough, at least for today. I found my way back through the front door and hopped into my Viper, ready to roll.

Instead of going home, I took a slight detour to The Hot Spot. It had become my new favorite hangout, and it was under new ownership. The former owner, a guy named Tiny Watson, took a bullet to the brain. He wasn't coming back from the grave any time soon. Since his brother was in the slammer, Dragon Lady, one of my new friends and not her real name, bought the place outright. She was better about saving money than I was—maybe she got her white t-shirts cheap.

34

Even though I hadn't seen her in about a month, she hadn't changed one bit. Her hair was still short, the fire was still in her eyes, and her shirts reflected light.

A long, L-shaped bar separated me from her, a live band had started jamming, the clientele had taken a step up, and the place no longer smelled like burnt popcorn. Blondes, brunettes, and redheads filled much of the available space, and she'd traded pretzels for peanuts.

I had high hopes, and I hoped they got even higher.

"Have you talked to everyone?" she asked. She didn't mean at the bar.

"Not yet. I'm working my way around. In my experience, you never learn it all the first time. When in doubt, conduct follow-up interviews. It's kind of strange the way life works—"

"How does it work?"

"You have to watch out for all the crap, because, if you don't, it sneaks up on you, and then you have to spend the rest of your days fighting your way out."

She popped a top on a bottle of beer and slid it down the bar, all in one motion. I tried not to be impressed. "I'd say your hopes are rather limited," she said.

I held a finger up to my lips. "Just don't tell anyone. I wouldn't want the secret to get out. I have a hard enough time the way it is. I'm more wanted than a terrorist on a jetliner headed straight for the Sears Tower."

"Are you here for a purpose?" she asked.

"I thought I'd see how you were doing . . . and to see if you wanted to go for another ride in my Viper. We could drive to Richmond and back." I meant the one in Virginia, not the one in California. I had no desire to live on the West Coast. The East Coast gave me more than enough problems, traffic being pretty high on the list.

"Are you going to let me drive?"

"Maybe next time," I said. "I'm still breaking it in." Though it was a 2005 Dodge Viper SRT-10, it had less than 40,000 miles.

"That's what you always say. Pretty soon you're going to run out of next times. For all I know you might decide to trade up one day, and then you'd have to find someone else to harass."

"I know, and I mean it, too." I didn't.

"One of these times you're going to have to say yes. I'll wear you down. I've got more staying power than gonorrhea."

I cringed. "You're welcome to wear me down any time you want. But you might want to close up the place first. You wouldn't want to have rowdy customers, seeing as how you're the new manager slash owner. You'd clear the place out faster than if I yelled 'Bomb!' at the top of my lungs."

Dragon Lady said, "You know I'm not interested in you, right?"

"Yeah, I know—"

"But you're going to continue to try anyway. You wouldn't even know how to give up. You'd keep swimming 'til you drowned."

"Actually, I'm an excellent swimmer," I said. "You have to learn how to fend for yourself after you do a face plant in the water. You start slapping the water for all you're worth, and, if you see a fin, you start slapping faster." I hadn't actually seen any fins or sharks, unless you count standing on the other side of the tank at Sea World and local aquariums. "I'm all about putting forth my best effort," I added. "It's important to know when to step up to the plate and swing for the fences."

She grabbed a mug in each fist and filled them up with Guinness and Harpoon. "And you also need to know when to take a walk."

"Are you kicking me out?" I asked. I sipped my Heineken and contemplated ordering another. I must not have contemplated hard enough.

"Not exactly. I just like to give you a hard time."

"That's my job," I said. "What do you know about professional dancing?"

"Personally?"

I nodded.

"Not very much. But my sister danced for years."

I waited for her to continue.

"It's what many young girls aspire to. It ends up being about as popular as cheerleading. Dancing is regimented, prestigious, disciplined, and competition at the top level is fierce. Women can be downright cruel to one another. At least with men, you beat the crap out of each other, shake hands, and then grab a beer. With women, we'll destroy your mind, body, and soul, in that order, and then we'll come after all the leftover scraps, in case there's something left. By the time we're finished with you, even your own mother wouldn't recognize you."

I asked, "Just how tough is competition at the top?"

"Very. Dancers have to be in top shape, they have to stay that way, and there is no room for injuries. Dancers and eating disorders go together about as well as models and eating disorders do."

"It's a good thing I'm on a steak-and-beer diet then." Although I did have my fair share of both items, it wasn't exactly true. The truth involved the women at the bar who seemed to be getting hotter by the minute. If the present trend continued, I'd have to hose myself off and then find a cot so I could spend the night. I'd already had two women resort to touching, and another woman grabbed my ass.

Dragon Lady didn't seem to notice. "Did you come here for anything else, or are you just admiring the view?"

I did like the view. "I thought I'd see how you were holding up."

"Well, I'm glad you care."

"Hey, you're one of my best sources of information," I said. "If I don't keep you happy, I'm in a world of hurt."

I explained the case to her.

"Your eyes are going to hurt tonight. You might want to pop them back in your head before you go." Another top was popped, and another beer sailed toward the end of the bar.

"What can you tell me about women?" I said.

"Well, that's more my specialty. In case you haven't noticed, I'm quite the expert. Women make a habit out of keeping you in line."

Not likely.

"I was hoping to learn about dead ones."

"You're not going to start screwing corpses, are you?"

I guess she didn't put anything past me. I couldn't say that I blamed her, but I didn't want to get the sick fantasies started. "No way, José—"

"Cuervo," she said. "Now you're speaking my language. I'll be right back."

A blonde nudged a big black man off the stool next to me, plopped her bright red drink on the bar, smiled, wiggled her butt, and then French kissed me, while hoots and hollers echoed around me. She winked, slipped me a piece of paper, grabbed her drink, and vanished in the crowd. I pocketed the paper without even looking at it.

When Dragon Lady returned, she shoved a glass of tequila in my direction.

"If you're going to get me drunk so you can drive my Viper, you're going to have to get a lot nastier than Jose Cuervo. My body metabolizes alcohol like it's Kool-Aid. I've already burned off my first bottle of Heineken."

"Yeah, that's what scares me. You're a machine, you have no moral code, and you like loose women. You're an accident waiting to happen."

I smiled. It was one of my better ones. I didn't lose a beat with my questions either. After all, I was a professional.

"Tell me, why would someone rush the cremation process? One way or another, they're going to get the body. A thorough analysis ensures the case is done properly."

"See, that's just it," she said. "You're assuming this is a normal case. Maybe the family wanted to put the past behind them; or maybe the victim had something to hide; or maybe the cremation is meant to cover up the sins of the victim or the family; or maybe the killer has friends in high places—or maybe the case wasn't *meant* to be done properly. And that's why they called in the cavalry."

"Is all that pure speculation?"

"Yeah, pretty much," she said. "It's something you're very good at doing as well. I try to learn from the best. It helps move things along in an expeditious manner, and it keeps you out of my hair—except on special occasions."

"Baby, I'm as special as they get."

Dragon Lady said, "Don't call me baby or I'll pinch you until you squeal."

"That would take a lot of pinching."

"So, do you think you're going to solve this one?"

"I solve everything," I said. "One way or another, I always get my man. I may have to play with fire, and I may get burned; or I may end up in a Dumpster; or I may end up with a bullet in my thigh or a knife in my side or a vision of the afterlife, right before I pass out on the ground—but that's all part of the experience. It's how you live that really counts, and I plan on taking life all the way to the finish line."

She said, "You're also a man who knows how to stick his head up his own ass. You should think about using your right foot to stomp on your left. That way, you'll get maximum efficiency out of your pain, and I won't have to look at a headless man."

7

After my tour of The Hot Spot, I headed for home with an extra number in my pocket, a smile on my face, and the promise of a better tomorrow. The promise rose like the American flag on a US Naval base. Dragon Lady provided answers for questions I hadn't even asked. Maybe the dragon on her neck provided a second brain. The case held more potential than a blonde knocking back a line of vodka shots.

At home I turned on The Point, a local rock station, grabbed a Heineken from the fridge, and headed for my black leather couch. Before I could get well acquainted with the couch, my cell phone rang. I slipped it out of my pocket and said, "Holden here."

"You're not going to like this . . ."

It was Isabel.

I took a deep breath, put my feet on my glass coffee table where they belonged, and waited. Nickelback filled in the blank spaces.

"Are you listening?"

"I am." I hoped the questions would increase in difficulty, otherwise I might fall asleep with my feet sticking out.

"Good," she said. "I didn't have to call you, and I didn't want to do what you asked, but I did."

If she had been next to me, I would have handed her a Girl Scout cookie. I had a box of Thin Mints shoved in the back of my freezer.

"Isabel," I said, "anything and everything you do for me—well, I appreciate it." Maybe I would nix the Girl Scout cookie. I didn't want to give her the wrong impression. Besides, I'd read somewhere that chocolate was an aphrodisiac. No, that's not right either: I'd have to give her two. Cookies, that is.

"That's more like it," she said. "I did it as a favor."

"And I appreciate it." In person, I could have further expressed my gratitude. "What did you learn—like it or not?"

"Jessica Mason died due to strangulation, and then she was placed elsewhere."

If this were a word puzzle, I'd vote for Scrabble. "You mean dropped off in the VDC parking lot, right?"

"Right," Isabel said. "But there's more. You'll never believe what happened."

"I'll try," I said. I had multiple talents, one of which was that I could conjure up images of naked redheads on command.

"The paperwork from the lab wasn't quite right, so I pointed it out to them. I retrieved her from the crematorium before it was too late."

Retrieved was the operative word. I had an image of Isabel performing the fireman's carry with Jessica Mason just as she was about to slide into the flames. My imagination helped me get through my more serious endeavors.

"Howard Brien at work again, huh?" I asked.

Isabel, though, was faster than my Viper on an open road. She ignored my question and said, "At the crematorium, the whole place was filled with dead bodies. I had to practically pry Jessica Mason away from Mort McAdams—you know, the guy who runs the place. Which reminds me. I gave Mort your cell number, and if he has any issues with what happened, he can take it up with you." She paused. "Just hang in here with me."

"I am," I said. I threaded my fingers at the back of my head, as I inched backward on the couch. "Take your time."

"Well, I thought Mort was going to have a heart attack right there in the middle of his basement over the whole business.

And then when I asked for his help transporting the deceased, he just laughed at me. I had to arrange to haul her out of there on my own. Casey, it smelled like someone had set a car on fire. I nearly gagged on yesterday's breakfast. You know me. I've never been callous about death."

"I know," I said. I could have conducted multiple consultations, with and without my couch and the dining room table. At one point, I'd considered becoming a consultation expert until I realized it wasn't a viable career field, and there was another term for it: psychology. Still, I had nearly reached expert status.

"Anyway, I got it all sorted out. I suggest you screen your phone calls. Mort might call you. He's so angry with me, he might try to take it out on you."

"Thanks, Isabel, it's the thought that counts." I chose the Teddy Roosevelt philosophy: speak softly and carry a big stick. I just needed to work on the speak softly part. Besides, I did owe Mort a whack or two for his multiple transgressions.

Silence followed. For a minute I thought I'd lost her. Or maybe she'd lost me. One could never tell these days. Then she said, "Are you all right, Casey?"

I stood up, stretched, took a sip of beer, and sat back down. "Yeah, I'm okay."

"Oh, good." I heard her take a deep breath. "There's more."

"I was hoping for more." Not all of my wishes came true, though.

"A partial fingerprint on the victim's right hand. We might have had a full one if Mort hadn't started applying makeup for a viewing before cremation. We'll run it through the database, and if we get any hits, I'll let you know. It's iffy, but a possibility. Oh, I almost forgot. FYI—there was a watch with a broken band near the body."

"Fibers?"

"No."

"Hairs?"

"He was careful, Casey. Killers are not always so careful. This one was fastidious, I'd say."

I'd have to look up fastidious for my next Scrabble tournament. "Why *he*?"

"A female wouldn't do that to another female. Further, a female would have to be strong enough to put her in a car and dump her at the VDC." She'd been dumped in the back corner of the VDC parking lot out of the limelight, or in this case, the overhead lights.

Maybe the fireman's carry wasn't so realistic after all. If I didn't have a fantasy, though, I'd be stuck in reality for the rest of my days. "Have you ever watched the WWE, boxing, karate on TV?"

"Okay, I get your point. But under normal circumstances females don't do that to other females. That's where the men come in. Males cause all the trouble."

That had been my experience as well. Men named Bradley and Sonny had proved especially difficult in the past. "I'll keep that in mind. Can you tell me anything else about the body?"

She said, "I can give you a time frame for her death."

"Shoot," I said. It was my favorite word—until some idiot actually took me seriously. And I'd met my share of idiots before, most of whom had either tried to outwit or outclass me. Many had tried; none had succeeded.

"When did you find her?" Isabel asked.

"I didn't find her."

"Oh, well, she died Friday evening or early Saturday morning between ten p.m. and two a.m."

"That's a pretty big window." All time of death did was allow me to work the alibis. I'd just have to question people, most of whom would be filled with all kinds of wonderful, useless information—until someone came up with a wrong answer.

"You'll get my full report tomorrow," Isabel said.

Click.

She had hung up on me . . . again.

8

When I got off the phone with Isabel, Alexandra popped over to say hello, and, despite good intentions, we both ended up naked. All in all it was a good night.

As for today, I hoped it would be even better. Dragon Lady had given me food for thought, but then there was my old flame . . .

Somewhere in the past there'd been a certain song, and I don't remember the artist, but it was all about an old flame and not even remembering her name. The bad part was I couldn't help thinking about her—and I knew her name . . . Isabel Titler.

I couldn't get that woman out of my mind. It was as if she'd moved in and planned to stay.

I sipped coffee, my feet on my desk, looked out my window at the brick wall, and tried to contemplate my next move. Until the Medical Examiner's report landed on my desk, which should be any minute now, I decided to banish Isabel from my mind and put in a call to Ian Jackard.

Ian is my best friend, sort of mentor, a nagger, who liked to snuff out every great idea I ever had. I opened with the proverbial, "Are we having fun yet?"

"That depends on what kind of fun you're having," Ian said. "My fun is rather limited at the moment."

"It always is for you," I said. I poured myself another cup of coffee. I had a feeling I was going to need it. The coffee stared back at me with soft, pleading eyes.

"I like it that way," he said.

"I'm not sure I'd call that living. I'd call it more like skirting around the edges of life. You've got a one-way ticket to Unpleasantville, and you may or may not know when you've arrived. If you're lucky, you might be able to ask for a refund."

"Your choices don't sound better, cowboy," Ian said. "You're one spur short of a full set."

Since I had never owned a spur, or even a cowboy hat, I was well short of the proper attire. "How would you like to do some detective work for me?" I might as well give it a try. With Ian, you never knew.

"Nicola says I need to stop. She says you're going to get me killed some day. Besides, the pay is for the birds. She says—"

Nicola was Ian's wife. She was a looker, and I had no idea why she put up with him.

"I don't believe you," I said. "That's *you* talking, and you know it."

"Well, it's true," he said, "no matter who's thinking or saying it. Listen up, Casey. Hearing screeching brakes as some nineteen-year-old kid slams into you, the twisting of metal, the popping of glass, the engine humming, that's when your life flashes before your eyes. That kind of shit just happens. But you—"

That was the first cuss word I'd heard from Ian in over a month. Having been gone, though, I could have missed a few.

"It does in my world too," I said. I tried to console him, but that would have been a full-time job, and I wasn't sure I was up to the challenge.

"Have you ever thought about how sick and twisted your world is? The crap that happens to you? And that's not the least of it. I mean, how many guys date two women at once and are always on the lookout for more? I'm surprised your eyes haven't popped out of their sockets."

"A guy can look, and you know it. What's more, I can touch and not get burned. Well, so far—"

"Knock it off," Ian said. "By now, you're not only skating on thin ice, but the ice is melting." He meant my nebulous relationship status.

I tried not to hear the words. But they were there. Well, okay. "Are you in or are you out?"

"What do I have to do?" he asked.

"I'm not sure. I'm just gathering evidence on this new case I'm working. I do need a second opinion on some things, possibly some leg work, and the names of the cops—other than Howard Brien—who processed the scene. And, no, I can't pay you."

"Do you expect something bad to happen to me? Like getting stabbed, shot, or hung from a banister in my underwear?"

"Don't remind me of the good ol' days," I said. One of my fondest memories involved Ian dressed like a woman. And he was not in his underwear, although he might as well have been, since a dress and pumps were his outfit of choice. Mine, not his. I only recalled it on special occasions, but there were many such occurrences.

"We don't have any 'good ol' days.'"

"If there were ever an optimist in you, he died a slow, painful death, possibly at conception," I said. "What kind of sick fantasies are you and Nicola engaged in? Maybe you should talk to a shrink. You may have some serious issues from your childhood you should examine. Who knows? But if you're trying to play mind games with me, it's not going to work."

"Some days I wonder just how smart you are, Casey. I really do. You're sane one minute and completely insane the next." He paused, and I heard him shuffle papers. "The names of the cops are Rick Stephens and Adam Mayberry. Don't cause more trouble than necessary. Some of us still work for a living."

My coffee was cold now. I looked out my window. The brick wall was still there.

The trouble with Ian was this: He had a conscience. I didn't. I leaned on him; he helped me stand up. He was the good guy, I was the bad guy. He'd been married twice, and he'd had only a handful of girlfriends in his life, and I kept women like spare parts to a car with the engine shifted into drive. But never mind. I thought about our past together . . .

Ian was the reason I became a cop. We met at James Madison University, and during his final semester we became friends. It was almost instantaneous, our relationship. Upon his graduation from college, he moved to Norfolk, and I didn't have anything better to do when I graduated three years later, so I followed him. I'd grown to like the Tidewater area, otherwise known as Virginia Beach with its surrounding suburbs. While I could have left, I decided the weather wasn't bad, I was close to the ocean, it didn't cost a fortune to live here, and I was just far enough below the Mason-Dixon line to notice. The traffic, however, could be downright vicious on I-64. It was a free-for-all, and I was lucky I had a big engine.

Finally I said, "Will you?

"What?"

"Do some work for me."

"Well, okay," Ian said, as if he couldn't refuse.

I took a quick glance out the window. The brick wall hadn't moved. I was getting good at persuading Ian to follow me anywhere.

"I want to discuss some things with you," I said.

"What?"

"Do you know anything about Jessica Mason's death?"

"No. Rick and Adam are working the case. Period. That means they've not invited me in. Which also means that you should be careful how and where you tread. You don't want to end up with two cops on your butt instead of one. There's only so much dodging, ducking, and avoiding you can do before you face the consequences." He sighed for additional emphasis. "Do you hear me?"

"I hear you," I said. It wasn't much. But it was better than nothing. We'd see how it all worked out. "It's just that I have this feeling that someone might have taken it upon themselves to start knocking off members of the Virginia Dance Company. Once there were fourteen, now there are thirteen. I may end up getting involved in conversations with all the beautiful women of the VDC and have to practice up on my sleeping skills." I could nod off at any time, not just special occasions.

"You could be right, but I doubt it," Ian said.

"I hope you're right. If I'm right, time is not on my side." Time was never on my side. The ticking clock had started a few days ago. "The guy who did Jessica Mason left no clues," I added.

"She could've been killed because somebody else wanted her place in the company or for a particular performance," Ian said. "That would rule out a guy."

I thought about that. "You make a good point. Or maybe she was killed by a lesbian who had misunderstood friendliness for something more. Or maybe a female owner wanted to be rid of a troublesome dancer. Or—"

"Strangulation focuses on power and aggression," Ian said, "and those are inherently male traits."

"Look," I said, "that may be true. But guys get into heated arguments, step outside the bar, beat the crap out of each other, and then head back inside and have a drink. Women, on the other hand, will fuck with your mind for years, possibly even decades and—"

"You just like to picture catfights with lots of moving parts."

"They're breasts, you moron. And they don't bounce that much. You get more action in basketball." Only Ian would use the term *moving parts* as a descriptive phrase for the female anatomy.

Silence. Ian was thinking it over.

I said, "You know something? You need serious help. Are you and Nicola doing the happy dance enough?"

He didn't answer.

I moved on, adding, "Isabel also thinks it's a man, but I'm still not convinced. I've been to the dance studio, and the ratio is skewed about seventy percent in favor of females. That means we have more female suspects than male."

"What if it's a jealous lover?" Ian said. "I've known a few jealous men who would slit the throat of the wife, the girlfriend, the other man—possibly all at once—and not even give it a second thought."

"And just happen to dump them all off at a ballet studio?" I said. "Men don't set foot anywhere near a ballet studio unless their girlfriend or wife has threatened their manhood—or they got lost and need to ask directions."

Ian said, "Nicola says I'd rather be lost than ask for directions."

"She's only teasing you, Ian." Nicola was good to him.

"I know. But some things are better left unsaid."

"How true," I said. "Did you ever tell Nicola that words can sometimes hurt?"

"No."

"Then you should." I was always eager to console Ian because of his ex-wife. I couldn't remember her name—come to think of it, I didn't want to. She had beaten him on a fairly regular basis, and he had never struck back. He had taken it and taken it . . . If she hadn't dumped him and shacked up with another man, Ian might still be a bruised and battered mess, sucking on Altoids, and waiting for his next therapy session.

Suddenly it was as if Ian had hung up the phone. Yet I could hear him breathing. "Are you okay, Ian?"

"Yes. I'm thinking. She may have been raped and murdered by an estranged fan."

"Isabel didn't find semen, hairs, or fibers. Only one-half of a fingerprint. Our killer might as well have been a ghost."

"The killer could've worn gloves."

"Did you ever hear of anyone wearing gloves while strangling someone to death?"

"Maybe he was wearing driving gloves. The killer wanted to be in complete control."

I gave up. Ian was a lost cause for the time being. I confirmed his desire to help, and he promised he would. With that, I told him I'd be in touch later.

Had I believed in breath mints, I would have gone in search of an Altoid.

9

My fire engine red Viper provided me with a certain amount of comfort as well as a certain amount of horsepower, uncommon in other vehicles. The engine purred like a cougar, and I felt as powerful as if I had a .44 Magnum in one hand and a machine gun in the other. I was Rambo without the weapons or the training—and I decided to take myself straight to the Virginia Beach PD. Unlike Rambo, I still had to operate within certain remnants of the law, although I had more leeway in my current position than in my previous one as a detective.

The place hadn't changed since my last visit there. The desks were still lined up in rows without the benefit of partitions. Keys clicked, phones rang, unruly guests shouted to be heard, and the place smelled of bleach. When the secretary, still as sexy as ever, winked at me, I knew I was in the right place for sure. She was a cougar, right down to the nail length, makeup, body, and dress code.

I didn't find Rick Stephens and Adam Mayberry. They found me. "So you're the PI who's been stepping on our toes?"

"Not me," I said. I could tap dance with the best of them, especially once I had a bit of rhythm flowing through my capillaries.

"Then what would you call doing a second autopsy?"

"Being thorough?"

"And stirring up trouble at the Virginia Dance Company?"

"Making progress?" I liked quizzes, especially the Trivial Pursuit variety. Scrabble didn't offer this much feedback.

Since Stephens and Mayberry weren't wearing name tags, I couldn't figure out which was which.

"And pissing off Kathryn Gable?"

I laughed. "The icing on my cake." I had a real knack for pissing off everyone, including clients. It was all included in my fee, and it gave my rates a nice, healthy bump. As for the two bumps in front of me, they were about the same size and age, with matching haircuts and tans, and they were too large for me to stomp on them and get it over with.

"This is our investigation," the one on the left informed me. His mouth was about the size of Texas and was his best weapon. It certainly wasn't the one in the holster dangling inside his sport coat.

"Well," I said, "since I was hired by Kathryn Gable, I'd call it my investigation. You boys are just along for the ride. You're doing this out of the goodness of your hearts, for your country—and the force should thank you for your service."

"We've been warned about you, and the warnings don't do you justice."

The force wasn't strong with the one on the left. "Great," I said. "You've hit the nail on the head. So, what can you tell me?"

"Do you ever read the papers?"

"Not on a regular basis," I said.

"You might want to start." And with that they turned and walked away in unison.

I sought out the sexy secretary and asked her if Ian was in. He wasn't. I decided Stephens and Mayberry were just another little mess I'd have to clean up later. Procrastination was the ultimate form of motivation.

I took my leave, opened my Viper's door, stepped inside, and tore away from the Virginia Beach PD with the radio blaring, my mind racing, and the cars in front of me inching along at a snail's pace. If

I had gotten out of my Viper and crawled, I would have returned to my office in half the time.

Before I greeted my leather chair properly or filled my coffee cup, Isabel stepped across my office door's threshold and dropped a file on my desk.

I looked up and said, "Isabel," and I didn't sound anything like myself. I sounded off, like I had a sparrow stuck in my throat and making a nest.

She was dressed in a silk shirt of pure cream and wearing beige linen slacks. With her blond hair, she looked like a million bucks—and I wasn't counting.

"I didn't plan to carry this to you," she said. "I just planned to have my secretary call you and tell you to pick it up. But you've not been sounding well at all. Are you sure you're okay?"

"I'm fine, really fine." What was the matter with me? Where was my snappy comeback? Maybe the bird had started looking for more straw.

Whereupon Isabel came around my desk, took hold of my wrist, pressed her fingers there, and after a moment or so said, "Your pulse is a bit rapid, Casey. Do you see a physician regularly?"

No, but I did have my stethoscope handy. It was in my bottom desk drawer with the spider web, minus the spider. "Not since that last case where I ended up in the hospital. But the doctor who saw me told me I was going to live forever—if someone didn't kill me first." I believed in the first part of the diagnosis, but I'd come perilously close to the second on more than one occasion.

Isabel's laugh was a whisper of sweetness, the honey variety. "I know what he meant," she said. "You probably ought to take better care of yourself. Someone told me they saw you at The Hot Spot recently, and you were drinking a Mexican Boilermaker."

"A what?"

"I think it's a shot of tequila washed down by a beer—or something like that. It sounds lethal to me."

To add to my ever expanding legend, I didn't correct her. "For you," I said, "it would be." The shot, however, had stood right where Dragon Lady had left it, guarding my bar stool.

She laughed again.

It was a long time since I'd heard that laugh, and it flowed like beer through a tap.

"Well, you know me," she said. "A little wine at dinner is about all I can take."

She smelled like a flower garden.

I almost said, "Let's give it one more try." But I didn't. For Isabel I imagined myself a different man, changed however subtly, and I didn't know how or where to start . . .

I took a deep breath. "Sit down. I'll give you a cup of coffee. Black. Like you like it."

She nodded, and then peered up at me through her eyelashes. "I've been so busy. I should take a minute for myself." She sat down in the chair across the desk and looked around the office. "You could use a bigger place and a window without a brick wall."

I fiddled with the coffee pot, unplugged it, and poured a cup for Isabel. "Watch your fingers," I said as I handed it to her.

"No problem. The cup's hot—not too hot. Thanks." She looked up at me and smiled, did the eyelash trick again.

I thought I was going to go down for the count right there. I took a deeper breath, straightened and said, "Now let me look at the final report." I sauntered around my desk, sat down in my leather chair, and opened the file. But I couldn't concentrate. The eyelash look slapped me harder than a former linebacker now masquerading as a bouncer and part-time thug.

I looked across at Isabel as she quietly drank her cup of coffee and thought about better times and better circumstances.

When she finished off the coffee she placed the cup on my desk. "I really must go," she said.

I nodded. My cup of coffee mocked me. I swallowed too much, scalding my tongue and the roof of my mouth in the process, but I stopped the laughing.

She rose from the chair. "Call me if you have questions."

I patted the file on my desk. "Any surprises?"

"There's probably a surprise or two in there." As she left, she called back to me. "It all depends on your definition of surprise."

10

Isabel was right.

When I opened the folder, I did find a couple of surprises.

First of all, Jessica had saliva in her vagina. Secondly, Jessica was pregnant. As for the partial fingerprint—no match.

What I had was a dead female dancer with short, raven hair, a heart tattoo on her left shoulder, and not an inch over five foot three. She had died of strangulation, and she had been dead for about an hour before she had been placed in the VDC's parking lot. Oh, and one other thing, a men's wristwatch—careless. Either that, or it could have been planted for obvious reasons.

It was time to ask more questions and hope for more answers. And the best place to stir up trouble was the Virginia Dance Company. So, I hopped behind the wheel of my Viper, the top down, the wind blowing through my gelled hair, and the sound of traffic surrounding me. Horns filled in the random bouts of silence.

I wheeled into the parking lot of the VDC to find the front door locked, darkened windows, and a sign informing me to proceed to Walkman Theatre around the corner. I raised the roof on my Viper, locked my car up tighter than a German bank, and walked around the corner, whistling on this fine, humid day and feeling optimistic. I didn't know why, except pessimistic wouldn't cut it. And my best friend was louder than Chicken Little with a megaphone.

I stepped inside the vast structure that was the Walkman Theatre, with its vintage sign, and I felt I had hopped into a time machine that turned back the clock about fifty years. The seats were oak with red velvet backing, the aisles stretched long and narrow, the stage was a large half oval, the balcony was wrapped all the way around the theatre, while all the molding was oak with gargoyles etched into the wood. A series of overhead lights on a large beam were focused on the stage, and the bulbs were various colors.

I chose a seat in the middle, with an open chair in front of me so I could put my feet up. It was best to observe in silence, since I was now surrounded by voices, classical music, and a promise of the past, so to speak.

I couldn't figure out exactly what they were doing on stage. They were wiggling and jiggling and moving, somewhat gracefully, all over the stage, both men and women with no regard to order, placement, or height. For specific periods of time their bodies seemed intertwined, and I couldn't figure out where one person ended and another began. They hopped, skipped, jumped, and slid across the stage. Each dancer ended up exactly where he or she needed to be, and no dancer struck another. Soft music flowed from the stage toward me.

Well, that was something all right. But *what* I couldn't guess. It all eluded me—the one with two left feet. Not to say I hadn't danced in high school, but that was slow dancing at the prom. And I did that only to get my arms around the girls as soon as possible and try to encourage them to go somewhere alone with me the next night, like the football field, underneath the bleachers, or parking in the middle of a forest.

I wasn't that old, was I? If not for my blown knee, I could have been a football star with lovely women flashing me at the forty yard line with the image projected on the Jumbotron. Was it truly possible that time was passing swiftly and I had no control over it?

I slumped in my seat and tried to watch the dancers at work. Bright, bouncy cheerleaders with perky extremities filled in a few of the blind spots. Finally I pulled myself together and focused my undivided attention on the stage and the curious direction of the case.

I could have sat there all day—in the audience, third row back, my hands behind my head and my legs spread as wide as space allowed.

Seat engineers evidently didn't take into account taller guys like me when they built airplanes, stadiums, and theatres. Being two inches over six feet, I was presented with all kinds of problems in my efforts to determine the optimum comfort level without jamming my knees into the wood. But without others in the audience now, I was free to adjust myself accordingly to accommodate the shortsightedness of builders and engineers.

The theatre definitely had a very old look and feel to it. I didn't find Abraham Lincoln sitting in a box seat overlooking the stage itself, but I was caught in a time warp that ran backward, fascinated by days long since passed, more so than with the dancers as I glanced around the place. About the time I realized the VDC had good taste in theatres, or smart financial backers, the music stopped, and the dancers disappeared from the stage.

I lowered my feet and scrunched down in my chair as I waited for the "second" act. I didn't want to be obvious, since one never knew when Kathryn Gable might arrive and banish me from the premises, or an as-yet-undetermined dancer might accost me in the middle of the theatre.

The music began again, and the dancers appeared looking as fresh as a new paint job, hopping, skipping, bending. The bending part was good, especially the women. I had been sidetracked on more than one occasion and failed to ask the most obvious question: How far can you bend over? A dancer with curly red hair bent like a pretzel and held the pose for a good five seconds. Without warning, I had developed a new shade of lust, bordering on the cherry tomato variety.

"So what do you think?" a male voice next to me asked.

I had been concentrating so much on the bending that I hadn't even noticed a guy arrive and sit in the seat beside me. The ace detective tried to look alive and on duty. If questioned further about the scenario, I would blame it on the bending. "Great, just great. I especially like ladies who can bend like pretzels. After the performance, I might have to visit the dressing room for an autograph. And finish my facility checklist." I patted my pocket.

The man didn't blink. "Most men do. It's not hard to get inside the male psyche. I could do it with my eyes closed and both hands tied behind my back."

Once upon a time the man had been tall and skinny, I suspected. Now he was tall and beginning to pack on the pounds, especially around the middle. He had graying short-curly hair, a long nose, and beady brown eyes.

In response to his remark, I said, "You mean I'm falling in step with the rest of the crowd? I can't have that. I'll have to change my way of thinking. I'm not sure what my attitude will be, but I'll come up with something. I need to focus on originality."

"Strange," he said.

"What?"

"You. You're a little strange. Odd. Different."

"Give me time to ponder—"

"What?" he asked.

"What you said about me being odd." I preferred the oddities of life, as opposed to slumming with the rest of the roosters.

"Oh . . ."

I gathered we had finished examining that issue, since one of his eyebrows had gotten away from the other.

Then he said, "You must be the private eye. I was told you might show up. I was also told your mouth would be larger than your body."

I wanted to hang one on his jaw. But I reconsidered. I thought of the redhead, good first impressions, and more bending. "Sometimes my mouth comes in handy. Just call me Casey."

No use in making an enemy. I already had enough of those, and I wasn't even really trying. Besides, he just might tell me things I wanted to know.

Sure enough, he stuck out his hand and said, "I'm the Virginia Dance Company's choreographer. My name's Ollie Nuber."

We shook hands. "Good to meet you," I said. "Those dancers on the stage are fantastic." I had visions of blondes, redheads, brunettes, and raven haired cuties all dancing and bending in unison.

"Well, thanks. I work hard at it."

"I'm sure you do. Personally I couldn't learn to dance like that. I have no rhythm." To make matters worse, I had dancing partners and physical education teachers to back me up on that point.

Ollie chuckled. "Rhythm can be taught. But I suppose not everyone wants to dance. It's a unique and inviting way to express yourself to the world."

I was interested. "Is it true that women are better dancers than men?"

"Not necessarily. It depends on passion. I've seen very few fail who had the passion to dance. Of course, some have more hope than others. It all depends on the individual and the commitment level."

I nodded and said, "Passion, huh?"

"Yep, passion," he said.

I kept an eye on the stage, and I was glad that I did. Kathryn had come on stage and joined the dancers. She was about ready to spill out the top of her lacy yellow costume. If I'd had a camera I'd have taken a picture. The thought crossed my mind that I ought to dump my old-fashioned cell phone and get one that a guy could take photos with. But I'd rebelled this long, no use in stopping now. Or maybe mine already had that feature and I had simply failed to learn how to use it.

Move ahead, I told myself, as Kathryn did a small step or two and twirled around the stage.

Then Ollie said, "You're cuter than I expected you to be. I've heard some of the women talking, It sounds like you're getting quite the reputation around here." He gave me the once over with those beady eyes. "You might want to watch out, though—or, then again, you might not."

And without another word or a goodbye, he stood up and moved back up the aisle, where he disappeared through the exit. Based on his previous comment, if he hadn't exited the stage, I would have done the task for him. I didn't have anything against being hit on—it's a nice ego boost—but I had work to do, and the dancing and bending were far more important.

11

After the performance I wandered back to the dressing rooms to see what kind of trouble I could find. I missed out on all the good stuff, but I did catch an errant boob and a pair of red panties before someone shoved me outside. The hand was soft, and the voice was firm—if that matters.

While hanging around to see what might develop, since naked flesh was not a write-in candidate, I ran into a dancer named Hailey Baker.

She asked if I might be the PI on the case.

I told her I was.

She smiled and told me I had potential.

I informed her I had lots of potential, and plenty of saddles, but she didn't seem interested in my saddles or horses, although she did seem rather keen on my potential. We were in business. I asked for her help.

"What kind of help?" she asked.

"Jessica Mason," I said.

"I knew Jess," Hailey said. "But I didn't know her well, you know. We hung out and stuff. But it was more because we had stuff in common."

Hailey wasn't a total ditz—I didn't think she was—but she was darn close. She stood on the fringes with the kiddie pool in close proximity.

"Like what?" I asked.

"Dance." She picked at a fingernail. "Boyfriends. She liked to get her nails done. Nails are important. Guys like that sort of thing, you know."

Nails were not a high priority with me, although I did seem to recall a rather large man and a pair of pliers. He had wanted me to talk, and I had wanted to keep my fingernails. I didn't recall the winner, although I might have blacked out somewhere in the middle of that process.

Still, Hailey needed a little encouragement. She'd already started her rather half-hearted performance, and she didn't even know it. That was the best kind of situation to be in, and I didn't want to exploit it too soon. In Casey's notebook, one rule stood out prominently: If someone wanted to talk, let 'em talk—in fact, encourage them to talk. And I'd been told by a string of ex-girlfriends that I had no problems in the encouragement department.

Hailey seemed primed and ready. She looked me up and down.

"You're not a dancer, though, are you?"

"Nope," I said. But I did enjoy the parts that involved stretching, bouncing, and of course, bending over.

"You like to watch, though?"

"True. It's all in the name of research, and I'm world-renowned for my thoroughness. I need to figure out ways to keep busy, or I'm liable to get in a bit of trouble."

"I've noticed you hanging around," she said. "And I've heard others talking about you."

"I hope they said something nice about me."

"You're not as silly as you think you are," she said.

"Good," I said. "I never set my expectations too high or I might be disappointed."

Hailey nodded her head vigorously. "I know, right?"

Her brown hair fell into her face; it couldn't keep up with her head.

I reached out and brushed it aside. I was trying to be good. I had my moments, and then I had my relapses. I never knew what would hit me at any given time. The relapses seemed to hit the hardest, though.

"Wow, maybe you really are a gentleman," she said. "Guess I shouldn't believe the stories."

I wanted to laugh, but I didn't. Oh, well. Despite having a chest that resembled that of a small boy, I tried to picture her naked. I couldn't. There were too many pretty women in the company, and I wanted to entertain every last one of them, though I wondered if I could go the distance, chest or no chest. I seemed to recall a running article on pacing oneself, but the details were rather murky.

She was wearing bright pink tights. It wasn't possible to get them any pinker or brighter. I didn't have my sunglasses handy. In such situations I should have come prepared. Once I'd worn my Oakley's on top of my head, but I'd adjusted my habit once my gelling phase kicked into fifth gear.

"Could you tell me about Jessica's boyfriend?" I asked, just as if we'd been talking about him. Catching an interviewee off-guard was also a part of my rules for success.

"Oh," she said, accommodating as all get out, "you know about him, huh?"

I could have kissed her. The dumb ones were the best ones to talk to. I was always surprised by how much information I could learn from stupid people. And the process always proved more enjoyable for all.

"Some," I said. "I'm counting on you to tell me all about him. After all, you and Jessica were friends."

She picked at a nail. "I'm gonna miss her," she said, staring at a point just above my head.

I noticed Hailey's nails were a bit ragged, the nails slightly uneven, especially her index finger and thumb. I tried not to hold it against her.

"I'm sure you will," I said.

Her lower lip protruded. "She was my friend," she said.

"And I'm sure you want to help me find answers to questions surrounding her demise. That's why I keep a note pad handy. To write down information." I slapped the back pocket of my jeans, as if that's where the note pad waited. "Right now, as far as I'm concerned, it's all for Jessica."

"I'll miss her," she said. The point above my head was back and in contention.

"Will you help me—knowing that it's all about Jessica?"

"I'll try," she said.

"What's his name?"

She scratched her left ear. "Whose name?"

She was dumber than a three-way stop. "The boyfriend."

"I don't have a boyfriend," she said and looked away.

I wanted to slap her cross-eyed. I'd just gone through a whole song and dance to prime her for what was to come. Yes, she was no Einstein. Not even his sister. Or even a distant cousin twice removed.

"Remember?" I asked. "This is all about Jessica."

"Oh, why didn't you just say so. You want to know Jess's boyfriend's name."

I nodded. "Right."

She looked up at the ceiling before earth came back into view. "Derrick Stevens. I thought you knew. He's the jealous type, though, so if you're figuring on talking to him, you might want to cover up first." I assumed she meant the t-shirt, or maybe she didn't.

I leaned forward and gave her a little peck on the cheek. I had this rule about kissing the opposite sex in public: It was highly encouraged under any circumstances and for all occasions.

"Thank you, Hailey."

"You shoulda just asked, and I would've told you right off." She blushed. It could have been related to the kiss or possibly her newfound intelligence. "You know, you're like the bodyguard we've never had. Will you be spending much time around here now?"

I nodded. "This is where all the action is."

"What action are you talking about?" a new voice asked.

I turned around and stared at a lithe woman with sharp, pinched features, wearing makeup applied in a haphazard manner, and lipstick that was a shade lighter than dark purple. Underneath the makeup, I could tell she was a reasonably attractive, older woman for whom years of dancing had been kind, even if the makeup hadn't. She had a toned look to her. I wanted to reach out and test my instincts.

I laughed and said, "I wanted to catch a glimpse of a stray breast or possibly a pair of lace panties. I never know when my eyesight might fail." Mine had been known to fail at the most inopportune times, although that could have been related to my propensity to get whacked over the head with foreign objects, or shoved out of women's restrooms for conducting random stall inspections.

She conducted a rather thorough review before focusing her rather intense gaze at my t-shirt. "Your eyes appear fine to me as does the rest of you. I'll bet you don't need any help when it comes to viewing the female form. However, if you're a pervert, I'll have you removed from the premises so fast your arm will pop out of its socket."

"I have a fault or two," I admitted, "but being a pervert isn't one of them."

She stuck out her hand. "I am Veronica Sutton, director of the VDC."

"Casey Holden, and I'm world-renowned for my offensive endeavors."

"How very appropriate, considering your wardrobe." My t-shirt read, NOTHING BEATS A BJ. The back referred to bungee jumping, but most women never made it that far.

"I'll have you know I put a lot of thought into my wardrobe. Great t-shirts don't come cheap."

Veronica said, "You and I have different definitions of greatness."

And with that Hailey broke into side-splitting laugher, and I decided I had been had by both of them.

12

"What the hell do you want?"

"I'm here to sell you Girl Scout cookies," I said. "Are you interested?" The cotton ball in my pocket, which I'd obtained from Hailey Baker before we parted ways, remained silent.

"I don't talk to wise guys." Derrick Stevens started to slam the door, but I was too quick. I caught it mid-slam and opened it back up again. That was one of the advantages to working out.

Derrick wasn't a hard man to track down. He was in the book, and all I had to do was whip out my pen and paper and copy down his address. I'd never visited his neighborhood before—I just pretended to know what I was doing. The houses were a bit older, some of them rundown, kids on skateboards sailed down the street, an ambulance let its siren rip, rap music blared from an old Cadillac, and a shabby looking guy began eyeing my car before I'd even hit the sidewalk.

"You're asking for trouble, buster," Derrick said.

"You're in luck—I have several middle names, and one of them is trouble. You're psychic. Do you have a crystal ball in your house? Maybe I should take a look."

"If you take one step inside my door, I'm going to take one step out and kick your ass," he said.

He used the door as his shield, but I didn't doubt for a minute that he would try. I didn't think he'd succeed. "You're pretty sassy for a short guy," I said. "Do you pack a mean punch in a small package, or are you just a small man with a small brain?"

"That's it. I've heard enough. Let's dance, you and I."

"Oh, I'm not very good at that," I said. "I haven't even started taking lessons yet. It could be next year before I even learn to waltz properly."

Derrick Stevens just stared at me. His mouth wasn't open. I was pretty sure he was trying to figure me out.

I've seen the look before, so I was used to it, and if he wasn't such a pain in the neck, I might have smiled. I figured if I could get him psyched up enough, I just might get some good information out of him.

"Just what exactly are you after?" he asked. He kept one hand on the door, just in case he had the opportunity to slam it in my face.

"I'm after a lot of things—women, peace on earth, a rich uncle—but I'll settle for information." I didn't want to set my expectations too high.

"Well, you've come to the wrong place. I don't give out anything, including information," Derrick said. He tried a smirk—it didn't work very well.

"Darn," I said, "and I thought you were a nice guy."

"Well, you thought wrong, dude."

I punched him in the mouth.

"That's assault, you bastard."

"I'm not a nice guy." I couldn't have Derrick thinking I was going to let him get off easy. "We can do this the easy way, or we can do this the hard way."

"I like hard," he said.

"I figured you would."

I jabbed my right fist six inches away from Derrick's nose, and I held it there, until he crossed his eyes.

"Hey, what are you trying to pull?" he asked.

"I don't want to have to hit you again, but I will." It was an empty threat—I don't think he noticed. "You tell me what I want to know, and I'll leave you alone. But if you mouth off to me again, I'm going to put you on your keister."

"Who uses the word keister?"

"I do," I said.

"Well, that's good to know. I suppose you go around beating up everybody."

"Just the people I don't like," I said.

"Bet that happens a lot."

"Not as often as you'd think," I said. "Most people are cooperative, or if they're not, at least they're nicer about it. I don't think you have it in you to be nice."

Derrick just glared at me. I could get into a staring contest with him, if I had the time to sit around and play games. I didn't. I had more important things to do—clues were at the top of my list—and they weren't going to appear out of nowhere.

"I'm beginning to think you're not a very nice guy. You're lucky I don't call the cops. I'm sure they'd like to hear all about you. You're probably some rogue agent with an inferiority complex, a quick temper, and a bad attitude."

"Well, what can I say?" I shrugged my shoulders to show Derrick my indifference to the matter. It was easy to be indifferent; having an opinion took much more work. I'd figured that out the hard way. Getting burned in a relationship did that to me. I didn't get burned under normal circumstances—my high school sweetheart got herself killed in a tragic accident. She'd been killed instantly, and the driver that caused her car to go out of control had walked away unscathed. That didn't sit too well with me.

"You don't plan on leaving, do you?" Derrick asked.

"Information first, leave later," I said. I didn't grunt like a caveman—it wasn't appropriate in this situation.

"You really are one giant pain in the butt," he said.

"You know I was just thinking the same thing about you. Great minds must think alike," I said. I didn't think for a second Derrick Stevens had half a brain.

"You need to work on your wit. And while you're at it you might want to fix your charm, too. The violence won't cut it with most people."

"Thanks for noticing," I said. "I'll put it at the top of my list."

He shook his head. I had a feeling this conversation was going to go nowhere fast. I decided to keep pressing anyway. He was the next roadblock, and I had to figure out a way to get past him.

"Tell me about Jessica Mason," I said.

"I don't know a Jessica Mason."

I balled my hand into a fist.

Derrick looked at my hand and tried to act tough. I saw him flinch first.

It's always best to go with your first instinct, so I played off of that. I didn't have much else to play off of, and I wasn't getting anywhere by being nice, so I decided to change the rules a bit. I liked to think of myself as flexible, even if I couldn't touch my toes. And I was pretty sure he wouldn't call the police—he just liked to scream loud. I'd known a few girls like that. The quiet ones always turned out to be the screamers. I happened to have a strong affinity for the quiet ones.

"Try again," I said.

He shoved on the door. When that didn't work, he decided to open his mouth. "Okay, man. I knew her, all right. We went out for a while, but it was nothing serious. I'm not even sure I remember her all that well."

Derrick was lying through his teeth. I wanted to be able to whistle through mine.

"That's it?" I asked. If that was the whole story, then I was a singing canary.

"Yeah," he said. He didn't even have the guts to look at me. He stared right past me out into the street.

"That's not what I've heard."

"What have you heard?" Derrick asked.

"I'm the one who's supposed to ask the questions."

"You're doing a lot of questioning," he said, "and I'm not even sure

I like you all that much." His voice had lost some of its forcefulness, and I knew I'd have better luck dancing than I would talking to him, so I decided to look elsewhere.

"Most people don't," I said. And then I walked away.

13

Before I peeled away from the curb, I pulled the cotton ball from my pocket with my left hand, used it to wipe my right hand, and then I placed it in my glove box for safekeeping.

I called Lana Ralstein before I even hit the highway.

"How did you get my number?" she asked.

"I'm a PI, remember?"

"Well, now that I have you on the line, can I take you out to dinner?"

"I thought you'd never ask," I said.

Lana lived in an older apartment complex five blocks from the studio. She told me she couldn't beat the commute time; however, the complex needed a bit of work. I couldn't agree more with her assessment. The trees and the siding appeared to have seen better days. She was the exact opposite of her surroundings: Her eyes sparkled; her lips were cherry red; her hair was pulled back from her face; and she had a devious smile. And she had gotten ready in less than twenty minutes: She was the woman of my dreams.

I drove Lana to Texas Roadhouse. It had large salads, a friendly staff, dancing girls, and steaks the size of Texas. I've heard that some of the skinniest women can have some of the biggest appetites. I wanted to put her to the test, without using up all of my charm in the process. I wasn't sure how much I had left.

She went for the salad. That didn't surprise me. She told me she needed to keep her figure. I tried telling her she looked just fine. It didn't work. Her self-confidence had been shot to hell, and she wouldn't tell me why. I didn't press the issue, because I had more pressing issues to get to the bottom of, and Jessica Mason was at the top of my list. It was a short list, with the potential to get longer, and the longer it got, the trickier things would get for me. If they got tricky enough, I'd have to start taking notes. I made it a habit not to take notes, and I made it a habit not to carry a note pad with me. I noticed people opened up more without the note pad, so I'd get back to my car before I jotted anything down, or if I left my note pad at the office, I'd go there first. It was a good system, so I stuck to it. I didn't have any trouble getting women to open up to me—I had a problem making them stop.

My car didn't know how to stop either. Lana wasn't as impressed with my Viper on the ride to Texas Roadhouse as I thought she would be. She was a little turned off that it had the same name as a vicious snake, and I tried to tell her that's another reason it appealed to me. She just turned up her nose and looked out the window. She wasn't impressed with its speed either. I still needed to figure out what impressed her, and I was running out of ideas. I decided to ask more questions over dinner—that was the only way I'd found to get answers.

"Are offensive t-shirts your thing?" she asked.

"Among others."

"I've known teenagers who do subtle better than you do. You might want to try it sometime." I left the comment untouched. "And jeans?"

"I like wearing t-shirts with interesting sayings, and jeans are comfortable," I said. "When I need to dress up, I throw on a sport coat. Then I look like a movie star. I'm going to give Brad Pitt a run for his money."

She smiled out of the side of her mouth. The look grew on me. "But then you can't see your interesting t-shirts."

"It's one of the downfalls of dressing up, but I'm willing to make the sacrifice when I need to," I said. "What sacrifices have you had to make?"

"To become a dancer?" Lana asked.

I nodded.

"I've had to battle eating disorders, both anorexia and bulimia. Don't look so shocked. Many dancers have eating disorders, and I'm just thankful I beat them." She scrunched up her nose—a rather cute one. "I have the usual problems with my feet: blackened toenails, rough skin, oddly shaped toes. But it's the price I pay for going on pointe. I'll probably have back problems later; they've already started to a certain extent. I have tendonitis in my ankles and knees."

"Why would anyone not want to be a dancer?"

"It has its good points," she said. "You can't replace the feeling of being on stage, the spotlight on you, the audience captivated by your every move, and executing a dance to perfection. There's always something that can be improved, obviously, but I set both my mind and body free when I dance. It's the price I pay for perfection. And if I had to do it all over again, I would, in a heartbeat. Dancing is as good as sex."

"That's pretty good." I decided not to continue with my elaboration.

She gave me another winning smile. "You're damn right it is."

Our waiter appeared out of nowhere with our meals, asked if we needed anything else, and then he shuffled off again. He'd told us his name when we first arrived—I couldn't remember it. He looked like a nice enough kid. I could have done without all the looks in Lana's direction, and he needed to work on keeping his mouth closed. He did, however, seem polite enough, for whatever it was worth.

"And Jessica?" I asked.

"Here I thought this was about me, and you were just warming me up to get to the good stuff." She stabbed a piece of lettuce and shoved it in her mouth.

I had a feeling we'd be here for a while—I was glad I liked looking at her.

"I do have a case to solve," I said. I'd decided to attack my steak—it was either the steer or me, and I wanted to win.

"You do, but that doesn't mean you can't play as well."

"I never said I couldn't."

She seemed to like that answer, because I got the full smile this time. I liked the way beautiful women smiled, and the ones who were open and knew exactly what they wanted intrigued me even more. It was hard not to like Lana. I had to keep reminding myself how cutthroat the dancing business really was, and that any one of the dancers could have been Jessica Mason's downfall.

"So, did Jessica have many friends?"

"Not as many as you'd think," Lana said. "She was close with Kathryn and me, and that's about it."

"About it?" I said. I'd eaten half my steak; Lana still had most of her salad. I waited. I had all the time in the world. If I ran out of steak, there were always plenty of peanuts and line dancing to keep me entertained.

Lana said, "She had a lover."

"You mean besides Derrick Stevens?" She nodded. "In the company?"

"Yes," she said. "Kathryn Gable."

I almost swallowed my fork. "Are you serious?"

"Casey, you have no idea how serious I am." Her eyes told me she wasn't lying, and her body screamed come and get me. I didn't think it was appropriate to jump across the table, so I stayed where I was.

"I guess that means they were more than just friends." I chewed a piece of steak, while Lana stared at a bed of lettuce, her fork hovering just above the plate, not ready to dive down just yet.

"I guess it does."

"Why didn't she tell me this?" I asked.

"It's not something you go around telling everyone. I didn't even know myself, until Jess told me. And that wasn't until she and Kathryn were having problems." She stabbed more lettuce and a crouton.

There wasn't a drop of dressing anywhere near her salad. I decided not to point this out for fear of alienating one of my better sources of gossip. It probably wouldn't have done me any good anyway. The best idea was to keep her talking.

"They were having problems?"

"Casey, you may be a little slow, but I know you're not that slow."

"This is all just a complete shock to me," I said. There were two pieces of steak left—I decided against going for both of them at once.

"It was to me, too, when I found out. And believe me it wasn't easy. Jess was a very private person and so is Kathryn. Kathryn can be a little hot tempered, but underneath it all, she's insecure. I think she uses her rough exterior to hide the way she feels inside. But"—she shrugged her shoulders—"I'm not a shrink."

"It sounds to me like you're doing just fine," I said. "So, why did Kathryn come to me?"

Lana scrunched up her nose for the second time. "I've been trying to figure that out myself. And I don't have any answers for you. Even though their relationship was on the rocks, you could see Kathryn still loved her." She stabbed a crouton, tomato, and lettuce all at once—she was going for some sort of record. "And I believe she still does. Love conquers everything."

"Or it can be your downfall," I said. Our waiter had taken my empty plate away, so my only choice was to stare at her—there were no dancing girls at the moment—and I needed to digest my steak before I decided to work on a few peanuts. I tried not to make it too obvious. I was pretty sure I was failing.

"You don't have to be a skeptic all the time."

"I'm not being skeptical," I said. "Just realistic. I don't want to get in over my head. There's a point where you're walking uphill in a windstorm, and I don't want to risk blowing myself into oblivion."

"I have a feeling you do anyway. You ride around without a saddle."

"Not on purpose, but it tends to happen." On Jessica's case I was still safe, I just didn't know how long it would last. I'd fallen off a building into a Dumpster in pursuit of my last suspect, so I was pretty sure I didn't want to go that route again. I needed to change things up a little. Maybe this time I could fall off a boat.

"And what do you do about it?" Lana asked.

"I fight my way out. Sometimes it takes a while, and sometimes I get to have a little fun in the process, but I always end up getting what I want. I'm a man of action."

"I believe you are." There was a slight twinkle in her eye. I could get used to the twinkle. It lit up half her face: The other half was the devil dancing in the moonlight.

"You've eaten only half your salad," I said.

"Their salads are huge, and I'm tired of you staring at me. Either you're going to do something about it, or you're going to take me home."

"Even if I wasn't that hungry, I could get three of those down and still have room for dessert." I put extra emphasis on dessert.

"Do you have that kind of appetite for other stuff, or just food?"

"Are you hitting on me, Ms. Ralstein?"

"Is that what they call it these days?" Her look said it all—she knew exactly what she was doing. Once again I decided against jumping across the table. I could exercise restraint when I needed to, I just preferred the alternative. Life was a whole lot easier when you rushed full speed ahead.

14

I dropped Lana back at her apartment, gave her the customary kiss good night, and then I went on my merry way. I decided to go for a drive because I had some new information to ponder, and I still needed to figure out how it all fit in. I couldn't believe that Jessica had two lovers: Derrick and Kathryn; she was a month pregnant, and so far, no one was the wiser. I had two cops, Mayberry and Stephens, on my butt; a man named Ollie Nuber wanted to grab my butt. I had conflicting emotions about Isabel; Ian thought it was a good idea to wear gloves while doing the nasty; and I needed to track down the owner of some errant saliva.

What concerned me most was the saliva. Either Jessica Mason got around, in which case I might have trouble tracking down all of her lovers, or the killer wanted me to think she liked to spread her legs, or saliva man was being set up to take the fall, or this case was screwy with a capital screw. I decided to reserve judgment until later, just in case I needed to start singing a different tune. And if the canaries came home, I wanted a new birdcage.

Since my head was spinning faster than an out of control washing machine, I decided I needed a bit of advice and a Heineken to help numb the brain cells. The Hot Spot was the only spot on my list, and I had my eye on my favorite bartender.

"Have you ever wondered why you get picked for your cases?" Dragon Lady asked.

"I always thought it was because of my charm."

"Doubtful," she said. "Highly doubtful. The more likely scenario is that they assume you're easily manipulated and that you're not as smart as the police."

"I was the police," I said.

"But you're not anymore. Maybe your habits have changed, maybe you're something less than you were, and maybe you're being set up to lose."

"That's what they hope anyway. However, they're in for the ride of their lives. I hope they checked the height requirement before they entered my roller-coaster of insanity. One way or another, I'm going to get the job done."

Dragon Lady said, "I know what you're capable of, without you even saying a word. I can see right through to your soul. And as messed up as your relationships are, and as messed up as your life seems to be, you're more than capable of finishing what you've started. In fact, I wouldn't expect anything less of you." She had a mixed drink in one hand and a beer bottle in the other. She slid both of them down the bar without spilling a drop.

"Why, thank you," I said. "That's probably one of the nicest things you've said to me."

"Just don't let it go to your head, or I reserve the right to take back everything I just said. I can't have you messing up a perfectly good situation."

"I can keep my head small."

"Like you can stick to one girl." She spun a mug in one hand, while she filled a pitcher of Bud with the other.

"Hey, I've done that. Granted, it was a long time ago, and it feels like another lifetime, but it's happened. I've seen stranger things develop."

"So are you going to change people's perceptions of you?"

Not on your life. "No, I'm going to leave things where they stand right now," I said. "Sooner or later, my work will speak for itself."

"Or you might never get the results you want."

"If that happens, then I'll find a way to deal with it. In the meantime, I'm not going to let my current momentum take a hit. I'm on a streak, and I didn't even have to run along the beach naked to do it."

"You don't have to go full speed ahead one hundred percent of the time."

"It helps me stay on track," I said.

"You're going to give yourself an ulcer."

"I can take an ulcer. What I can't take is losing. Life is too short to experience loss. What I need are a few more success tokens."

"Why do guys always feel like they have something to prove?"

"Because we often do," I said. I drained my bottle of Heineken, while she made her rounds at the bar.

The clientele hadn't reached its beauty peak yet, but I still had at least an hour to kill before my curfew. If I didn't walk out with at least one phone number, it was a slow night. I could deal with slow nights; slow women were a whole other story.

I headed for the jukebox, and when I headed back to the bar, a blonde had commandeered my seat. She'd also commandeered my bottle.

"What do you think you're doing?" I asked.

"What does a girl have to do to get lucky around here?" She spun around, and I stared right into the beautiful gray eyes of Beverly Elmond, my second girlfriend. In the girlfriend business, it's always a good idea to have spares. She looked me up, down, and all around. If I had been a shy guy, I would've blushed at least half a dozen times; instead, I hadn't even blushed once.

"Well, not as much as you'd think," I said. "How did you know I was here?"

She winked at me. "Lucky guess."

"Are you following me?"

She deep-throated my bottle. "Maybe. Are you going to follow me home?"

"Definitely."

"Great," she said. Then she hopped off the stool, slapped my butt, laughed, gave me one of her famous pouts, and then she was a hop, skip, and a jump out the door.

Before, I could go, though, I had a few questions I still needed answered.

"You really know to pick 'em," Dragon Lady said.

I shrugged. "I'm a man of many talents."

"I'm sure you are, Romeo. What else can I get you besides another bottle? You look like you have something on your mind. And it's not women. I'd know that look anywhere."

"Well, I found out Jessica had two lovers, not just one: Her baby bump was a month along. I'd like to track down the owner of a saliva sample. I have a male choreographer who wants to lick away all of my gooey goodness. And I have two cops who'd like nothing better than to pound me into the ground."

"And you thought you had problems. Why don't you tackle it one issue at a time?"

I said, "That's my plan. I'm going to focus on the saliva sample first."

"It sounds to me like you've found a few reasons why someone might want Jessica Mason dead. Now, you just need to figure out if they're related, or which one actually caused her death."

"Or maybe it was something else entirely. And I just haven't discovered it yet."

She had a glass in one hand and a clean towel in the other. "You're even smarter than you look."

15

I had gotten up early, done my customary sit-ups and push-ups, showered, dressed, and was in my office before I was even fully awake. I had my second cup of coffee in front of me, so my eyes no longer drooped. My hall mate Mandy Humphrey, with her office directly across from mine, had yet to show her pretty face, and I had phone calls to make before my train of thought escaped me.

Through one cell phone call, minus any pleading, I convinced Isabel Titler to grace me with her presence.

Before she even had a chance to sit down, I stated my business. "I need you to compare a saliva sample for me to the one you retrieved from Jessica Mason's body." I handed her a cotton ball.

She stared at it for a minute, and then her mouth curved inward. "And how did you acquire this sample?" she asked.

"I'm not at liberty to say."

"Casey, did you obtain this sample through illegal means?"

"I punched a guy in the face," I said. "But he deserved it."

"I'll pretend I didn't hear that. And you can pretend you might actually have a decent bone or two in your body."

I smiled; she didn't.

She said, "I'll get back with you in about two hours."

"I'm looking forward to it," I said.

"You know, for a second there, you almost had me convinced."

I decided it wasn't too early for my third cup of coffee. After I had my feet back up on my desk, I leaned back in my chair, and downed a quarter of my third cup before I called Ian.

"Hey, I need you to do me a favor," I said.

Ian said, "I'm not in the favor-granting business."

"Is your long-term memory going? They say that's one of the first signs of old age."

"Actually, the short-term memory is the first thing to go."

"Wow, you're even worse off than I thought," I said. "I need to see Howard Brien's ME report."

"Why?"

"So I can compare it to the one I already have. I want to see what the discrepancies are."

"Is this because Stephens and Mayberry chewed you out?" He meant Rick Stephens and Adam Mayberry. Two cops who could pass for Munchkins.

"No, I just want to be thorough." *However, the thought had crossed my mind.*

Ian signed off sounding grumpy, and the next thought that crossed my mind was the dance studio. I still had unfinished business, and I was a few cards short of a full deck. But with a little time and a few willing bodies, I planned to have more answers than I had right now. If nothing else, it would be a good start to nailing down the truth before the truth nailed me.

"So just how friendly were you and Jessica Mason?" I asked Kathryn Gable. I wasn't one to mince words; I didn't have time to start up idle chit-chat; and I had a pretty good feeling she was withholding information from me. As a matter of principle, most people did. Cops, PIs, anyone with a badge or a license had to deal with less than full disclosure. Most marriages also went through the same spells. Yet another reason for me to never tie the knot. The thought of being told less than the truth on a regular basis, outside of my job, didn't sound like my idea of fun.

"We've already been through this," she said. She had a towel in her hand, which she used to wipe sweat from her face. She didn't have as much sweat as I would have thought. Her scowl had enough strength behind it for two men.

"Well, I'd like to go through it again," I said. "I've found out more information, I've gathered more clues, and I'd like to be able to tie everything together. Handcuffs are optional; full disclosure isn't."

"Why are you giving me the third degree?"

When answers are in doubt, always fire back with your own question. "Why didn't you tell me you and Jessica were lovers?"

To her credit, Kathryn didn't try to deny it. "I didn't think it was necessary. My personal relationship with Jess had nothing to do with her death. She and I kept our relationship discreet, and it remained separate from our dancing lives. The majority of the company didn't even know we were a couple."

"That's substantial information," I said. "In the wrong hands it could make things ugly. If you're like me, you just want answers. And your relationship may have had everything to do with her death. I've known jealous lovers to kill for less. And while you may have kept it discreet, suspicions arise, dance members notice subtleties you may not even be aware of, and there were folks who knew what was going on. No matter how hard you try to avoid it, personal relationships affect your work relationships and vice versa."

"Wow, detective, do you psychoanalyze everyone you talk to, or am I just getting special treatment? If you have a sofa handy, maybe I should lie down."

I didn't bother to correct her on the detective bit. It did have a certain ring to it. Old jobs die a slow, painful death. The memories of my former life startle me at the darnedest of times.

"That wouldn't be a good idea," I said. "I'm liable to take advantage of the situation."

She winked at me. "I wouldn't expect anything less of you."

I said, "Is there anything else you care to share with me in the interest of full disclosure?"

"Jess and I weren't lovers recently. We'd had a falling out."

"Over what?"

"She wanted to be closer than I was willing to commit to," Kathryn said. "And she could be a little flighty. That made me nervous. She was a good person, detective, but she wasn't the one for me. We were two different people." She paused. "We fought all the time, and it transferred onto the dance floor. It's better if you don't mix business with pleasure: I learned that the hard way. Little spats become big spats when you have to see the person at work *and* at home. There's no personal space."

The waiting room of the studio never felt smaller, and neither of us had bothered to sit down. I'd snuck up on her, and that didn't make her any happier to see me. Kathryn tried to keep a safe distance between us despite my best efforts to close the gap. Her sofa comment had thrown me for a loop, but not too much of one. I could read women better than most men, yet my radar still had a glitch from time to time. Frequenting bars helped me practice my moves, and it also ensured I kept up with the latest trends.

The tights showed off her muscular legs. I didn't think she had the habit of taking her clothes off—I stared at her just in case she changed her mind. I had this habit of trying to undress beautiful women with my eyes. All guys have it, some are worse than others, and some are just happy to be in the game. I had it bad, but I tried to keep it all in perspective.

"Tell me more about Jessica," I said. "It sounds like you knew her best."

"She'd been a member of the Virginia Dance Company for three years, one year less than me; she grew up in Williamsburg, went to college at William & Mary where she studied dance; she was a bit on the shy side; her heart was as big as three of my fists; and she always thought she would fly some day. But her optimism wasn't contagious.

She was a very private person, detective. She separated her personal and professional lives as much as possible."

"Why would anyone want to kill her?" I'd asked the question of Lana before, but I didn't get an answer then, and when in doubt, I kept asking questions until I got the answers I wanted. Persistence was the key to success. There's no such thing as too much persistence.

"I can't figure that out either. She didn't have a single enemy in the world. Dancing was her life, and she was good at it."

When most things don't make sense, it's been my experience that there's a reason behind it, and when it appeared someone was hiding something, they probably were. I just had to figure out what it was. Depending on how good they were at lies and deception, it could be hard to figure out. That didn't keep me from trying. I knew the effort would pay off eventually, and when I evened the score, all would be right with the world—until the next fiasco.

"But someone wanted her dead."

"How do you know she was murdered?"

"I have my sources," I said. It's always safer not to convey more than I need to get the job done. Too much information just stirs up trouble, and I was already doing enough of that on my own.

Kathryn asked, "You conducted your own autopsy, didn't you?"

"I did. Do you want to hear what else I learned?"

"Sure, why not? You pumped me for information; I might as well pump you. It's your turn to lie on the sofa. Just don't throw your arms up in the air and squeal."

"I don't squeal, and I don't beg. But what I can tell you is we found a man's watch at the scene, still tracking down that lead, and Jessica had a heart tattoo on her back."

"You needed an autopsy to tell you that?"

"There was what I assume to be male saliva in her vagina; she had two lovers, you and Derrick, hopefully at different times; I had a run-in with the two cops working the case—Rick Stephens and Adam Mayberry—and let's just say I'm not going to put them on my Christmas list this year; her parents and the other dancers seem to have a fond opinion of her; I'm tracking down a lead on the saliva; and I have a contact who will get me a copy of the other autopsy report."

"Why do you need a second report?"

I said, "Let's just say I don't trust the guy who conducted the initial one."

"Do you trust anyone?"

I winked at her. "Not if I can help it."

16

I said, "Did you know she was pregnant?"

Kathryn opened her mouth, closed it, and then opened it again.

"I'll take that as a no," I said, right before I walked away. I went for the shock-and-awe factor first, and I liked to know more than the people I interviewed, just in case I needed an advantage. I'd found that it made life simpler, and in most cases, easier.

After our testosterone-fueled first encounter, I had no idea what I'd get from talking to Bradley again, but I knew it couldn't hurt, and I just happened to be in the area. If you let it, life often takes interesting turns.

"Why do I get the feeling you're withholding information from me?" I asked.

I'd found Bradley Cassidy, and it was better than any opening I'd used so far today. Plus, I wanted to watch the man squirm, even if he was straighter than a new dollar bill. He had on tights, a smirk, and a headband, and I had a feeling he knew how to use all three. Despite my best effort not to, I had caught him in mid-stretch, with his right leg high in the air and his hands near his ankle.

"You know," he said, "I could say the same thing about you." He stood on one side of the hallway, and I stood on the other. All I needed was a bigger gun.

"What are you still doing here?" I asked. Even though it would have been better to just walk away, I lacked a certain amount of willpower.

"I'd ask you the same thing," he said.

"I'm here for information, and right now, I can't think of a better place to be. If you happen to think of one, let me know." The snowball had started rolling downhill, and I needed to outrun it in a hurry. Maybe I should start making a list.

"Maybe you should give up now and save yourself a lot of time."

"There are causes bigger than me. And I don't give up. In fact, I'm just getting started. You haven't even seen my A game yet."

Bradley said, "On that, I think I'll pass."

"That's a nice watch," I said. "Is it new?"

"Yes, it is, as a matter of fact. I misplaced the other one."

I'd looked up *misplaced* in the dictionary when I was younger, and I happened to remember that it was another word for *lost*. While I may have been a little behind the power curve, I wasn't all the way at the starting gate either.

"You didn't happen to lose any saliva recently, did you?"

"What are you talking about?"

"Oh, I have no idea. Sometimes I just say the darnedest things. It's funny how interesting cases always bring out my strangest qualities."

Bradley said, "I'd say being strange is a normal occurrence for you."

"You know, you may, in fact, be right."

As he walked away, Bradley shook his head. I hoped he didn't have the headband on too tight. I wouldn't want it to start cutting off the oxygen to his brain.

I decided to wander around the studio and see what other characters happened to pop up. It reminded me of a carnival funhouse: I never knew what I might find.

On the third door, on the wing with the offices, I struck gold.

"I see you discovered a new t-shirt," Veronica Sutton said. She had on a lighter shade of lipstick, and the makeup was more manageable. Her eyes leaned toward suspicious.

My t-shirt was an oldie but goodie: It showed condoms playing musical instruments.

"Care to tell me what you are doing here this time? You certainly aren't dressed like an auditor who has randomly lost his way; you'd give accountants a bad name."

"I'm looking for naked women," I said. "You don't happen to know where I can find a few, do you?"

"Are you some kind of comedian, or are you just lost on a regular basis? I do not appreciate random men wandering around my studio."

"No, I'm a PI. You might have heard of me. I have a reputation that grows by leaps and bounds."

"Probably like your t-shirt collection. No, actually, I have not." She paused. "And what do you think you're doing? Obviously, you're not here to dance, and you are not here about a lawsuit, since I haven't been sued in over ten years."

"I'm just observing the talent." My 20/20 vision never mattered so much. What I could've really used was X-ray vision.

"Maybe you should conduct your observations elsewhere. I do not want my studio under some sort of microscope. What I need are fewer distractions, not more. And your t-shirts are loud enough to be heard in West Virginia."

"I've been hired by the VDC to track down Jessica Mason's killer. And I don't stop until I get my man . . . or woman. It helps to remain gender neutral, and while I don't require it, I'd certainly prefer your cooperation."

"Our company never hired you."

"Well, I had a meeting with Kathryn Gable two days ago, two days after Jessica's death, and I was asked to look into her untimely demise. And you're saying you had nothing to do with it?"

"Wow, you're fast. That's exactly what I'm saying, and all new hires would have to come through me for approval. In fact, I still hire a lot of the employees myself. We're a small company, and I like the personal, hands-on approach."

"So do I," I said. "In fact, the more hands on, the better. One can never get too personal these days. So you're a one-stop approval shop?"

She shuffled a stack of papers on her desk. "Apparently, word gets around fast."

"No, I'm good," I said. "It's my job to know what's going on."

"One will never accuse you of being modest."

I said, "No, one won't. Modesty is highly overrated: I've been cutting back for years, and I still have more to go."

I leaned on her door; she continued to shuffle papers on her desk; I ran my other hand through my spiked hair; she tapped the keys on her computer in rapid succession; and I studied the various original paintings on her walls, which were in stark contrast to the waiting room and long corridor.

After several minutes, she looked up.

"Is there something else I can help you with?" she asked.

"Yeah, did you know one of your dancers was pregnant?"

"No," Veronica said, "I had no idea."

If not for a slight twitch of the eye, she'd have been one of the best actresses I'd ever encountered. But I was trained to notice the subtleties, and the twitch was a dead giveaway.

17

"What did you say to Stephens and Mayberry? I haven't seen them this pissed since one of the other detectives, who shall remain nameless, Super-Glued all their office supplies to their cubicles. I've never laughed so hard in my life."

"Ian, are you telling me you actually laughed?"

"Don't try to change the subject on me," he said.

"Oh, it was no big deal. I think they're blowing it out of proportion. We just had a little chat about the Jessica Mason case. I got the impression they wanted me to stop snooping around. But since I'd been paid to start snooping, I can't go back on my word."

"Casey, I have to work with them. Not to mention the fact that if they really wanted to, they could have you arrested."

"What's the charge, detective?"

Ian said, "I'm sure they can come up with something. You seem to have at least one felony in the process of conducting an investigation."

"Actually, my latest one would be more of the misdemeanor variety. I punched Derrick Stevens in the mouth, but he deserved it, and it was for a good cause."

"What happened exactly?"

He asked, so I answered. After I was done, there was a short pause on the other end of the line. I used the downtime to focus on my driving. Despite the beliefs of most SUV drivers, their cars did not have invisible barriers surrounding their vehicles.

Ian asked, "Can you go one day without getting into trouble?"

"I can. But it's extremely hard to go several days in a row. That requires more talent than I seem to possess."

"Where are you headed?" he asked.

"Back to my office. I've had enough fun at the studio, and I have more information I need to process in the sanctity of my barren workplace."

"Good. Because I'm coming over."

Ian hung up before I could tell him to bring the tea and crumpets. I'd just have to settle for coffee instead. Maybe the jolt of caffeine would do me some good.

Somewhere in the middle of my second cup of coffee, Ian bounded through my door, tossed the ME report—the one with Howard Brien's signature on every other page—on my desk, hopped in one of my two client chairs, and before I even had a chance to respond, he'd hopped up again.

"I take it you don't need any caffeine," I said.

"Casey, that stuff's going to kill you."

"Better that than the two thousand other ways to die. However, number one on my list is still sex with a beautiful blonde. I could go out with the biggest smile you've ever seen."

Ian said, "You always did want to leave a big impression."

"So what does the ME report say?"

"Maybe you should read it yourself."

So I did. And while I read, Ian hopped up and sat back down four or five times. That would have been a personal low for him, so I was almost certain I'd missed a few.

"There's no mention of the pregnancy or the saliva," I said.

Ian nodded. "Maybe Howard just forgot to put them in his report."

"Or maybe he was paid to leave them out."

"Maybe he just got a little sloppy, since he's overworked and underpaid, and he didn't notice some of the finer details."

"Ian, you give the man way too much credit."

"And you don't give him enough."

"Have you given any more thought to the single life? You and I could make some serious waves in this town—after we got a few courtesy drinks in you."

"I like being married," Ian said. "The process of being divorced holds absolutely no appeal to me whatsoever. I need stability."

"You would," I said. Ian and I had differing opinions on a lot of topics. Sex and relationships hovered somewhere near the top of the list.

"Are you saying you don't recommend it? Since when have I listened to you anyway? You're just trying to choke my chicken."

"Don't you mean 'get your goat'?" I asked. Ian wasn't very good with the euphemisms. It didn't stop him from trying. And it didn't stop me from laughing. I still had my feet up, and I still had my unfinished cup of coffee in front of me.

"Yeah, that too."

"Ian, I've never met anyone as lost as you, and I've met a lot of people in my life." It didn't matter that most of them were women, and it didn't really matter that I'd slept with most of them. There were two kinds of women: the ones you wanted to sleep with and the ones you didn't. I just happened to focus on the ones in the first category, and I did my best to avoid the ones in the second.

"You mean women," Ian said.

"It's hard to tie yourself down to just one. I mean, there's an ocean full of options, and I'm fishing on a pier with two lines. And if I had three hands, I'd have a third one."

"Most people use one. It's easier, you don't have to pay quite as much attention, and you're less likely to let a good fish get away."

"That isn't nearly as much fun," I said. "It works better when you're trying to catch twice as many fish. There's a whole ocean of possibilities, and I want to experience them all. I'd rather not be caught holding just one line."

Ian hopped up and sat back down; I refilled my coffee cup; he peered out my door; I looked out my window, the brick wall winking back at me; he shook his head; and I smiled. It was a fair and even trade, and I decided to hold all the bargaining chips.

I first met Ian on one of my better days, when my right hook packed an extra wallop. He and I fought over a girl—I can't even remember her name or what she looked like—he was a senior, and I was a freshman. She was a cheerleader with the best legs this side of the Mississippi, and she didn't end up dating either one of us once she found out about the fight. I probably never would have spoken to Ian again—I hadn't really spoken to him much before that—but he sought me out and apologized. I was about ready to punch him again, and then I figured out he was serious.

"So are you finding out anything interesting?" Ian asked.

"You mean besides the pregnancy issue?" Which I'd already told him about, and which he didn't seem the least bit shocked by. Then again, nothing shocked Ian, other than his ex-wife leaving him. Even when I left the Virginia Beach PD, he had a look of cool, calm collection on his face.

Ian nodded.

"Well, Bradley has a new watch."

"Since when do you notice what men are wearing?"

"Since I started being a cop," I said. Before Ian could add that I stopped being one, I plowed ahead. "There was a man's watch left at the crime scene, and while it could be nothing, it does seem a tad bit convenient. I have Isabel—"

"Wow, I'm impressed she's still talking to you."

"—checking on a saliva sample for me. That's my misdemeanor." I paused. "It must be my charm." I then filled Ian in on all my latest assumptions, observations, and conversations.

He nodded occasionally, stood up often, and interrupted very little.

"So do you have any suspects?"

"That's the problem," I said. "At this point, everyone seems to be a suspect. Everyone I've met has either lied to me, withheld information, has significant character flaws, or is just plain crazy. I'm the only sane person on this case."

Ian said, "Stephens and Mayberry are still tracking down leads."

"I know," I said, "and that scares me more than all the Looney Tunes I've encountered over the past three days."

18

"Define Looney Tunes," I said. I'd been talking to Isabel Titler for the past ten minutes via my office phone, and she'd told me I deserved to be behind bars. I told her she probably wasn't far from the truth, but it would take more than her strong will to get me there.

"You're beyond crazy," she said.

"I thought I was on my way to normalcy." I also thought it might be normal for her and me to renew our relationship.

"Not by a long shot." I heard a bit of longing in her voice, or maybe it was just my wishful thinking. Every woman deserved to have a Casey in their lives.

I said, "Well, what have you got for me?" I referred to the cotton swab that contained the DNA of Derrick Stevens, but I might as well have focused on our current relationship. Or, as memory served me correctly, our previous one.

"You've got a whole lot of nothing. Which could very well describe the extent of my feelings for you at this very moment. I know you'd like me lusting after you, and while you may want more action than you're currently getting, you don't stand a chance."

"Great," I said. "I kind of hoped this would be an easy one." I could have said the same thing about her and that whole lust factor.

However, she was far from easy, and my case was far from over.

"Casey, you may consider yourself a sex machine, but you are never easy."

"I have more questions for you."

Isabel said, "This could be construed as harassment. Why can't you contact me during normal business hours?"

"I happen to fall outside the norm."

"That's what worries me. You only have a finite number of lives. And I'm liable to go after a few of them myself."

"I thought you'd say 'intrigued.'" I had my feet up on my desk, and I had my coffee cup in front of me fully fueled. All I needed was a t-shirt to broadcast my intentions to the world. Wait, I had that too: It referred to strippers *and* single moms. I figured both deserved my full support.

"Maybe I would have," she said. "But that was a long time ago, and you and I have both aged a few years since then. One of us faster than the other one."

"I'm glad you're willing to admit it," I said. "They say admission is the first step to acceptance. And once you reach acceptance, you're well on your way to a full recovery."

"And I'd say you were full of crap, but you already know that. In fact, I wouldn't be surprised if you were just trying to push my buttons."

I took a swig of wake-up juice. "Is it going to work?"

"Maybe in another lifetime."

I said, "Maybe we have a lot of lifetimes left."

"Is there a purpose to this phone call? Or should I call up the police and have you reported? Maybe you could even take a trip downtown." It was an empty threat, at least I hoped so anyway. After what I'd seen her do in a previous life—I once saw her flip off a cop—I wouldn't put anything past her.

I pondered that for a moment. I'd already gotten in enough trouble without the help of a scorched ex-girlfriend, even one I still had feelings for. What I needed were ways to circumvent the trouble scenario. My talents didn't extend quite that far; however, I still had talents even I hadn't found yet.

"How hard would it be for a cop to tamper with a scene?" I asked.

"It'd depend on the cop, and it'd depend on the scene."

"What about Jessica Mason's scene?"

"It's possible. While most of the bruises and contusions are consistent with strangulation and dumping a body, the watch and saliva are a tad bit convenient for my tastes. If not a crooked cop, then a crooked individual who's watched a little too much CSI could have done the same job. Said individual would have to cover his tracks well, remain unnoticed throughout the ordeal, plant the watch and saliva—which must have been handy in the first place—and have known about the scene before the cops got there."

"So it would have to be the killer," I said, "or someone close to the killer? And you said *his*." I tried not to miss a thing; sometimes it even worked.

"Exactly," she said. "You aren't planning on tampering with a few crime scenes, are you? That'd be a surefire way to have them revoke your license."

"I'm just entertaining a theory," I said.

"You always entertain theories. Do they ever get you anywhere?"

"Once in a while," I said. "You never know when you might actually pass through the brick wall."

"On a regular basis?"

"Not as often as I'd like. But then I always set high expectations for myself. I never know when I might actually do well enough to succeed."

"Why doesn't that surprise me?"

"Because you know me better than most," I said.

"Now that's scary," Isabel said. "I might have to sleep with the lights on tonight. And I'd rather renege most of those privileges. Your current girlfriends—I'm sure it's plural, not singular—should eventually figure you out. And when they do, you're going to have a lot of explaining to do. You'll wish you were out on the ocean, with the board between your thighs, instead of some woman's three inch heel."

"We were good together once."

"The key being once," she said. "Things change. You and I have changed. And in your case, I wouldn't say it was for the better."

"One of these days I'm going to become a man."

"I hope I'm around long enough to see it," Isabel said.

My desk drawer contained the slip of paper I had received from the blonde with the bright red lipstick at the bar, and her kiss still lingered on my lips. It was a good kiss: She tasted like raspberries and cream. The mental image of her had faded, but I knew I could get it back.

Before I could entertain theories of beautiful, naked women who had a thing for me, I needed to talk to a woman with a good head on her shoulders, who held no specific attachment to me other than my vehicle, and who threatened to disown me if I didn't let her drive my Dodge Viper SRT-10 in the near future. I'd have to put off the inevitable for as long as possible. But I had a big mouth, an even bigger brain, and I was used to dealing with women, even the difficult ones.

"What kind of man becomes a dancer?"

"An athletic man," Dragon Lady said. She had on a white t-shirt, her short hair was now red, and she had her usual pose: a glass in one hand and a towel in the other. She had used the towel to clean off at least one glass that I knew of.

The Heineken stared at me, and I stared back at it. Since I had two eyes, I figured I had the slight edge. "Are certain guys predisposed to dancing?"

"No, not particularly," she said. "Not all male dancers are gay. But a higher percentage of them are gay. However, quite a few of them are straight as well. Dancers are performers, the same way actors are performers."

"But nobody ever accused Brad Pitt of being gay," I said. I was sandwiched in between a blonde and a brunette; however, my existence had yet to be acknowledged. If I didn't have more important matters to attend to, I could have changed their outlook. As it was, I focused all of my attention at a woman who didn't want me. Life always had a cruel trick or two up its sleeve.

She said, "He'd certainly break a lot of ladies' hearts if he was." She set the clean glass down and picked up another.

"What about you?"

"I hold no strong affiliation for Brad Pitt. He's too much of a pretty boy for me."

"So you go for the bad boys?" I asked.

"We're not going to discuss my personal life. You, on the other hand, have a wide variety of relationships that we could discuss. We could spend hours without even cracking the surface. You have a sexual complex that has yet to be identified."

"I have no problem discussing my relationships."

"Maybe another time," Dragon Lady said. She flipped two drinks toward the end of the bar, grabbed a metal shaker, poured in three different bottles, shook it, dumped the contents in a glass, and then walked toward the opposite end of the bar.

While she chatted with customers, some friendly, some not, I paced myself on my first bottle. I was almost to the end, and I wasn't sure if I needed another. I thought about flipping a coin, but I decided I shouldn't leave drinking to chance. I might end up with one or two more drinks than I needed, and I didn't want my performance affected later.

The blonde and the brunette remained mute.

Dragon Lady returned.

I said, "So why do men dance?"

"For the same reasons they play football, join the band, the army, or the peace corps," she said. "They want to be part of a group, they're good at it, they like performing for an audience, or they want to stay in shape. Dancing is a perfectly acceptable profession."

"For a woman, yes."

"You need to leave your stereotypes at the door. Life is too short to face it with constant judgment. Men are more than just jocks, and women are more than just the occasional arm candy. Some of us even know what we're doing."

"I don't know any other way to be," I said. Even though I did have one or two good ideas, I decided I wasn't into expanding my particular notions.

"Now I know you're lying."

"Well, I could call them fairies." Even though I probably should have, I never did believe in the Tooth Fairy, the Easter Bunny, or Santa Claus. I had a warped childhood, and it had only gotten worse with age.

"And I could throw you out on your behind and slam the door in your face."

"You don't exactly have a whole slew of patrons lined up to take my place." The crowd had started to pick up; the band had started tuning their axes; the women, however, were in need of some serious makeovers. What they needed was an injection of fun.

"Do I look like I'm doing this for the money?"

"Then why do you do it?" I asked.

"Because I'm good at it, I'm a good listener, I enjoy the conversation and the company, I'm a people person, and I meet a wide variety of customers."

"And you get to dispense advice once in a while."

"Which I'm good at," Dragon Lady said.

"You don't need to get a big head."

"I wouldn't dream of it."

I had a particular fondness for my dreams, especially the vivid, graphic ones. None of them, however, contained Dragon Lady naked.

"How likely is it that a cop would tamper with a scene?"

"I don't know," she said. "You were a cop once. What do you think?"

"I'd say it would depend on the cop."

"And I'd say you were right."

"I think I might be back to square one," I said. "I have a saliva sample with no positive ID; I have a pregnant dancer who may or may not have told anyone she was pregnant; I've been told by the director herself I wasn't hired by the VDC; Bradley Cassidy has a new watch, because his other one mysteriously disappeared; Howard Brien fudged his ME report; and I have two cops who don't believe in information sharing."

"Sometimes you have to start from the beginning again to reach the end."

"You're not making any sense," I said. But I found out later she had made perfect sense.

19

What I did need to do was leap into bed. And I had a blonde who was ready and willing, and her name wasn't Beverly Elmond.

I reread her note. Along with her phone number, it read: How big is your pole?

"Who is this?" she asked.

"It's your wildest fantasy."

"I don't have any wild fantasies." Her voice was smooth, sultry, and with the slightest hint of honey.

"You do now," I said.

I told her my name, and then she told me hers. After five minutes she agreed to meet me, after another twenty minutes I talked her into going to her place, five minutes after that I talked her out of her clothes, and as they say, half an hour later the rest was history. I left a note on her pillow, telling her my pole was big enough, planted a kiss on her forehead, slipped my clothes back on, the piece of paper back in my pocket, and then I was out the door.

My day started off much the same as all the others. I had a few threads I needed to unravel a little more; I had coffee; I thought about the previous day's events, my sexual escapades being high on the list; and

I decided it would behoove me to do more serious detective work. As much as I didn't care about Howard Brien, I knew I needed to figure out where he had gone wrong, and I knew he wouldn't take it well.

For a pre-game warm up, I learned about bisexuality. In the span of a half hour, I learned bisexual women didn't always stay bisexual; instead, they maintained a fairly steady attraction to both sexes, and eventually they ended up in long-term monogamous relationships. As with all other pieces of information, I filed it away for future reference; however, at the moment, it wasn't of much use to me. Women, however, always were, and there were never enough of them to go around. I was glad I was always on the lookout for new recruits. I never knew where life would take me, but most of the time it was somewhere worth going.

With thirteen dancers in the Virginia Dance Company and nine of them female, I figured that was a pretty good ratio. I didn't get those odds in college. At James Madison University there were more females than males—it was one of the reasons I chose the school—but it was only by an eight percent margin. At the time I didn't know any better. Now I knew I needed to aim a little higher.

I needed to make a call, and unfortunately, he was male, with a high-pitched voice. It wasn't going to be one of my more pleasant conversations.

"Why are you calling me?" he asked.

I'd already told him my name, and that was the thanks I had gotten. If I hadn't been a phone call away, I would have probably taken a swing at him. As it was, I settled for a hand stamp on my desk. It appeared to enjoy the abuse, thus the sturdy wood and the deep red color.

"I need some information, and you're next on my list." I didn't bother to ask him if he had a few minutes, because I knew the answer would be no. My goal was to get as much information out of him as I could before I heard a click.

"What do you want?" Howard asked.

"I want some answers, and you're going to give them to me." I paused to let him ponder the situation. I didn't hear a click. So either

I was being recorded, he was going to repeat everything I said five minutes later, or he was going to help me. If I were a betting man, I would have gone with one of the first two options.

"Why did you conveniently leave out some information from Jessica Mason's crime scene? There's no mention of her pregnancy or the saliva in her vagina."

"I didn't leave out any information. It simply wasn't there."

I had my feet up on my desk. I stretched my toes, refilled my brew, and peered out the window. The brick wall might have winked back at me. "Are you saying that someone planted the saliva and knocked her up after she was already dead? That'd certainly be one out-of-body experience. Even I'm not that good, and I'm darn near amazing."

"No, I'm saying you got your facts wrong."

"Howie, now I know you're lying to me, because I never get my facts wrong."

"If you ever call me Howie again, it'll be the last word you ever utter."

And then Howard Brien hung up on me.

I didn't exactly want to talk to him anymore either. He was near the top of the list of my least favorite people. The only two who were higher were Rick Stephens and Adam Mayberry, and it had nothing to do with their physical size, just as Howard's had nothing to do with his high-pitched voice.

While I may not have known much, I knew Howard didn't have an honest bone in his body, and he'd sell his soul to the devil for a glazed doughnut. I also knew I'd need to get a few more facts lined up in my corner if I was ever going to put this case, all the beautiful dancers, and my lack of rhythm behind me. What I needed to do was hold my breath, puff my cheeks out, and hope for the best.

Before I looked like a two-year-old in the middle of a temper tantrum, I spotted my office mate across the hall.

"You know I've never properly welcomed you to the neighbor-hood," I said.

"Casey, if you're the welcoming committee, you're liable to scare off all the little kids," Mandy Humphrey said. She was all legs, tits, and ass, with flaming red hair and a flaming body to match it. Her abs probably could have cracked walnuts, and if her skirt were any higher, I could have seen the sun, moon, and the stars.

We'd had a few conversations, a few flirtations, no confrontations, and to my chagrin, neither of us had ended up naked yet. I would have raised six hands if I had them to vote for her, but I would have settled for myself as the naked one.

I flashed her my best grin. I said, "How come you and I have never gone out?"

She winked. "That's because you've never asked."

"So if I ask, I shall receive?"

"Maybe," she said. "But I wouldn't count on it just yet."

Before I could ask her what my odds were, she vanished down the hallway, and I was left staring at an empty door.

It didn't take long for more company to appear, and it wasn't the naked woman kind either. What I wanted to know, though, was where I had gone wrong. Maybe I should have said my prayers last night before I went to bed. Although, more than likely, even that wouldn't have helped my cause.

20

"What do you two want?" I asked. I was staring at the faces of Rick Stephens and Adam Mayberry, and I didn't like what I saw. Unfortunately, I didn't have a refundable ticket.

"We're here to take you downtown," the one on the left said.

"Do I need to pay my respects to someone?"

"No, but you could start by losing the smartass attitude."

"I only have one attitude," I said, "and it's focused on being smart."

"Well, you're focused on getting yourself in some trouble. You need to learn to keep your mouth shut, your eyes faced forward, and your hands off of our case. You also need to learn that harassing dancers isn't a full-contact sport."

"It wouldn't be the first time I was misunderstood."

"Is that what you think this is all about?"

"It has to be," I said. "Otherwise, you two wouldn't have shown up at my office."

"You're trampling on our case; you're sticking your nose where it doesn't belong; you have Howard Brien in panic attack mode."

"He's not a hard one to fluster. I didn't realize it was your case now. Did you get the same invitation to the party I received?"

"Yes, but ours has first dibs written all over it. At best, you get sloppy seconds. But what you should get is nothing and like it."

"This isn't high school," I said. "You two need to stop overreacting. We're both playing for the same team, and, if anything, we should be sharing information, roasting marshmallows, and drinking a few beers."

"You could have fooled me," the one on the left said. I was pretty sure he was Mayberry, and I knew I didn't like him. What I also knew was this: The conversation would have been a whole lot better for me if I hadn't been blindsided by two men with self-esteem issues and inferiority complexes.

"And it's not a popularity contest. This case is about finding answers, but I get the feeling most of the folks would rather cover it up. What I'd like to know is why."

"If it were, we'd win it," the one I thought was Mayberry said. "You'd be stuck in second-to-last place."

They never did tell me their leads, and I didn't expect them to. What I didn't expect was being handcuffed, stuffed in the back of a police car, and driven in the direction of downtown.

"I happen to like bringing up the rear," I said. "Am I really that much of a threat to ya'll that you need to take me downtown?"

"Maybe you are, and maybe you're not," Mayberry said. "But we have enough to fingerprint you, stuff you in a cell, and make your life miserable for a few hours."

Stephens, on the other hand, chose not to comment on much of anything. I wondered if I should ask him about the weather, just to bring him into the conversation. I wouldn't want him to feel left out.

"What kind of answer is that?" I asked.

"The answer one of your inquiries normally turns up. You might want to focus on how to conduct an interrogation. You go for the balls first; you hit 'em high; you hit 'em low; and then you leave them breathless. It helps when you know more than the people you're interrogating."

I didn't like the insinuation. "Have you been following me?"

"Maybe," Mayberry said. "But you're not much fun to watch. Although you do get more action than most porn stars." He paused. "We're paid to act. Not to think."

"That's where I come in. I'm the brains of this operation."

"You're the liability," Stephens said. And when we were there, he marched me right through the front door. I didn't stop; I didn't get to pass go; and I certainly didn't get to collect my two hundred dollars.

I was dropped in a holding cell with a concrete floor, a toilet that didn't flush, black metal bars with streaks of silver, and claw marks on the wall.

Stephens departed. Mayberry, however, remained behind. He had the ready-to-punch-me look written all over his face. His hands were balled into fists; his Adam's apple throbbed; a vein pulsed on his forehead; and his lower lip twitched.

I said, "Do I get my phone call?"

"Who are you going to call? Ghostbusters?"

"You know, that would have been funny twenty years ago," I said. "You need to keep up with the changing times. You're a little out of the loop, which may be why your investigation is going nowhere." I didn't know that for sure, but if they had the manpower to follow me, then they certainly weren't making good use of their resources. I was the least suspicious man in this whole operation, and I was the only one who had even begun to have a clue.

"You need to get a sense of humor," he said.

"I already have one of those," I said, "and it helps me through some tricky situations. You, on the other hand, probably never had one."

When he didn't respond, I plowed ahead. Since I was already in the slammer, I figured my situation could only improve. "It helps if you relax. You might want to try coughing."

He just shook his head. "Five minutes. You're not done, we're coming back to get you, and we're not going to be so nice the second time around."

"I didn't realize you were nice the first go 'round. You might want to look up what nice actually means."

Mayberry said, "I could grab your neck and squeeze."

I could never figure out why I always brought out the worst in people. Maybe it was because I was the best, and I always knew exactly what I was doing. Well, most of the time anyway.

I decided to help him change the subject. "The phone call?" I requested as nicely as I knew how.

Mayberry shrugged, gave me an evil grin, motioned for me to follow him, and took me to the phone just down the hall. There he left me in the hands of a guard.

I called (using a black rotary dial phone that was at least fifteen years old) one of the only people I could think of who might actually come to get me. I could have called a few women to have sex in prison. Even though I was into extreme sports, that seemed a tad out of my league. My twin bunk wasn't big enough for what I had in mind.

When Ian realized who was calling, he said, "Why are you calling me at this hour?"

"I need a ride."

"You always need a ride," he said. "For a person who drives an eighty thousand dollar automobile, you sure don't know how to keep track of it. Maybe you need to get a bigger beeper, or you could always gain a bit more responsibility."

"I'm in jail," I said.

"What are you doing there?" he asked.

"I'm doing calisthenics in the men's shower."

"Just make sure you don't drop the soap."

I tapped the wall, and then I glared at the guard who was skinnier than a metal post and even less friendly.

He glared back.

"Just make sure you get down here and pick me up," I told Ian. "I need to extricate myself from this situation before Stephens decides to get friendly."

"One of these days you're going to run out of favors."

As far as I was concerned, I had a never-ending supply. "And one of these days you might stop being a nice guy. On both accounts, I find it hard to believe. You don't have the heart to turn me down."

"I can be mean," he said.

"Ian, you don't stand a chance."

112 GRACEFUL IMMORTALITY

The guard yanked the phone from my grasp and hung it up.

Luckily, I was done with my conversation; otherwise, I would have needed to give him a lesson in civility. Maybe he could have taken a few notes, and, in the process, actually learned something useful. It was my job to educate the world, and there were a whole lot of folks who needed to go back to school.

Back in my cell, I did push-ups and sit-ups until Ian showed up. I did just over 500 of each, and I felt friskier than ever.

Ian arranged to free me from my cell.

As we walked out to his car, Ian asked, "What is it with you and jail cells?"

"We seem to get along a little too well."

"You can't seem to stay out of trouble long enough to come over to the good side."

"That'd require too much work," I said. "I like to take the easy way out. It's much safer, quicker, and efficient. Plus, I could always use a few extra style points."

Ian just shook his head. "So should I even ask? Or am I better off not knowing exactly what you did. That way if you end up in jail again, I can always plead ignorance."

"I've been a bad boy," I said. "Mayberry and Stephens aren't my biggest fans. In fact, they're not even in my top one hundred."

"Since when have you ever been a good boy?"

"I have my moments," I said. "I've been known to leave flowers or notes to the women I've bedded. I could own my own flower shop, or maybe I should go after Bic."

"There's also a lot of time that passes between your moments. You need to work on upping the ante." He paused, opened the passenger door to his old wreck and added, "Get in."

I got in, closed the door, waited for Ian to get behind the wheel, and kept talking. "That's open to interpretation," I said.

"So what did you do this time?"

"I was snooping around, asking questions that needed to be answered, and then I called Howard Brien to get a few details from his ME report. The next thing I know Mayberry and Stephens are in my office, they're pumping me for information, and then I find out I've been followed. The cuffs were bad enough, but now I feel completely and totally violated."

Ian tapped his chin. "You're always snooping around, and for some strange reason, you live for controversy. If it weren't for people like Adam Mayberry and Rick Stephens, you wouldn't even be able to function in society." He turned the key in the ignition, and we were off in more ways than one.

I wanted to argue with Ian about how well I function in society, but the point would have been lost on him. "Apparently, I'm not supposed to gather information. Maybe I'm supposed to flip myself over and stick my feet up in the air."

"I have a feeling there's more to this story . . ."

"Well, somebody at the dance company filed a report against me. The report said I was harassing dancers during a performance rehearsal."

"Were you?"

"Not exactly," I said. "I waited until the rehearsal was over, and then I hung outside the dressing room. I figured I had a good shot at catching an errant boob. My luck ran out, though, before I was able to catch the really good stuff."

Ian shook his head. "You should really work on trying to make something out of your life. Glimpsing breasts while on the job isn't exactly what I would call a success story. You should aim for something just a little bit higher."

"You haven't seen what I've seen," I said. And there wasn't a chance in hell he ever would. That probably had something to do with his resentment factor.

We arrived in front of the building where my office with its cozy leather chair awaited.

21

I'd spent most of my day downtown. Rather than chase after stars, I decided it would be better to chase after naked ones. Alexandra Bridges just happened to be naked enough for me, and we got an early enough start that we were able to go four rounds instead of our usual two or three. She was caked in sweat, and I still tried to entertain the possibility of a fifth round. She cut me off, got up, walked to the shower, sashaying the whole way, while I lay there, hoping to summon the strength to get up. I just didn't have it in me.

We both slept well, I got up, dressed, left a note, with a single flower—that I borrowed from the neighbor's garden—and then headed out the door, before I started thinking with my other head.

Since I hadn't worked off all my energy last night, I ran, did my customary sit-ups and push-ups, and even tossed in a few sprints, just to mix things up a bit. After that, it was time to ask a few questions and get a few answers. I decided to start with Kathryn Gable, and as always, I knew just where to find her. She stopped me in the waiting room before I'd taken three steps inside the studio.

"I don't see how your line of questioning is relevant," Kathryn said.

It wasn't a good time to point out that it was my job to investigate, and it was her job to provide answers. As long as each of us understood our duties, the process would go much smoother.

Like a good boy I'd come back for more, and I was getting it right across the chin. I could have sworn she could smell me coming. Maybe I had missed the little red light that had alerted her to my presence.

"I don't expect you to," I said. "What I do expect, though, is for you to be up front with me, and I'm a bit concerned since I spoke with Veronica Sutton."

"That was two days ago."

"I spent most of yesterday downtown. I managed to get myself locked up."

"How did you manage that?" she asked.

"Let's just say I don't have friends in high places at the moment. There's also the matter of a harassment complaint. Plus, I always manage to piss off one or two cops."

"But you were a cop."

"That'd be one of the reasons I'm not anymore."

She didn't know what to say to my comment. It wasn't the first time I'd left a woman speechless, and I knew it wouldn't be the last. I managed to take their breath away every single day, yet I still didn't have as much success with women as I would have liked. There was always room for improvement, even for someone like me.

"It might help all of us if you're a bit less intrusive," Kathryn said. "We still have a show to run, and you're taking up too much of our time. I appreciate what you're trying to do and how you're trying to do it, but there's got to be a better way. This case is a high priority for us, but if the show doesn't go on as scheduled, we could lose the studio. I'm sure you can see our predicament here."

Her right hand tapped her thigh—I tried not to notice.

I'd developed the impression that she liked to argue, and she liked to get under my skin. I hoped it was a valid assessment.

"I'm not asking for your help," I said. In fact, I wasn't quite sure what I was asking for. I just knew I wanted to find the truth, and I wasn't getting it. I probably should have taken notes. I didn't. Now I'd have to deal with the consequences. And they were aimed right at my forehead. It was a good thing Kathryn didn't have a gun.

"Then what are you asking for?"

"I'm asking for your cooperation. Why didn't you tell me the VDC didn't hire me? You led me to believe I was working directly for the studio. Since I'm not working for them, I'll have to assume I'm working for you, and what I still don't know is why."

Her hand tapped even faster; her mind turned over and over; and I wondered whether or not I would get a straight answer.

"I couldn't. You're still going to get paid. I cared about Jessica Mason deeply, more than I could ever express in words. She was my life, my love, my everything. While she may have been with another, I knew it meant nothing compared to what we had. Plus, the VDC has a history. There was an unsolved murder that took place fourteen years ago."

"I didn't know that . . ."

"That's because you weren't looking for it."

I nodded. Maybe I just needed a new kind of motivation, and maybe I'd found it. "Was it another dancer, and was the dancer female?"

"That's two questions," she said, "and the answer to both is yes."

I didn't know she had been keeping track. "How do you know me so well?"

"Casey, you're not all that hard to figure out."

"Wow, I didn't realize I was that transparent. I need to step up my game."

Her hand calmed down. "You have all the game you need." She whipped around and marched off before I could question her about the other dancer.

I wandered around the studio, taking inventory as I went. I made a mental checklist of the beautiful women, the ones I'd talked to and the ones I hadn't. Fortunately, the list of the ones I had talked to was longer than the ones I hadn't. I peeked in on a class, had a door slammed in my face, bumped into two beautiful women on purpose—however, I made it look like an accident—apologized, and then I slammed into

Lana Ralstein: a chest-to-chest encounter. Before I could tell her how sorry I was, she yanked me into an empty rehearsal room and closed the door.

Lana said, "You might want to watch where you're going, cowboy."

"I always watch where I'm going," I said. "I just don't always know where it's going to take me. Maybe one day I'll figure it out."

Before I could run for cover, she flipped on the light, spun me around, and took off her top. She had on a t-shirt underneath, but the desired effect remained the same: She got every bit of my attention. Even if I had wanted to take off, it would have been physically impossible.

When she informed me she would teach me how to dance or she would die trying, I laughed. "I can't even move both feet at the same time. How are you going to teach me to dance? Are you sure you have enough time on your hands?"

The rehearsal room was bigger than my living room, the floor was cherry, mirrors were lined up on the right wall, and various posters lined the other walls, most of them advertising dance. The room smelled of sweat, competition, and hard work. A jazz tune, possibly by Miles Davis, spoke to me from speakers in the ceiling.

I'd already stepped on Lana's toes three times, just to prove I didn't know what I was doing. I hadn't done it on purpose, and she hadn't screamed out in pain, so we were off to a better start than I'd expected. Being a man of no rhythm, I wasn't expecting much, so if I learned even two steps out of this, I'd consider myself saved. Maybe I could get one of those shirts they passed out at amusement parks after one of their giant roller coasters. It would read: I SURVIVED MY FIRST DANCE LESSON, AND I STILL HAVE ALL OF MY TOES. Like the rest of my outfits, I'd wear it loud and proud and with every bit of ego I could muster up.

Lana stared at me as if I weren't even there. I figured that was pretty hard to do considering I was a sex god and women practically threw their panties at me. I had on one of my killer smiles, but she wasn't swooning yet. I smiled wider. It still didn't work. I waited for her eyes to glaze over. They didn't. It took a lot of work to look this good—almost ten minutes had passed—and I didn't like to go unnoticed. It just didn't seem civilized. I knew women who spent less time in the bathroom than I did. I wouldn't have gone out with any of them; I just knew they were there.

She stepped on one of my feet. "I can teach anyone to dance, twinkle toes. You can step on my feet all you want, but you're not going to scare me away."

"My toes don't twinkle," I said. "I'm lucky I can walk without falling down. If I'm able to walk and chew gum at the same time, it's a good day." That was a bit of an exaggeration. I could walk and chew gum, or walk and talk on the phone, or walk and push a cart at the same time. In at least one case, I'd been able to do all four at once.

"You don't try hard enough."

"If I tried any harder, I might pass out from sheer exhaustion."

"You have more hot air than you know what to do with," Lana said. She had on pink tights and a cute little pink skirt. I tried not to think about what was underneath the skirt.

"You're not going to try to corrupt me, are you? If you are, you might want to get a bigger stick. And you should probably lose the outfit. You might want to go with a leather top, a cowboy hat, three inch heels, and nothing else."

"Are you here to learn, or are you here to cause trouble?" she asked. Her tone said she didn't want to play games—I was a big fan of games. Tonsil hockey was one of my favorite sports. I had passed the novice stage long ago, and I had long since deemed myself an expert.

"I was hoping for a little of both," I said. "Are we not supposed to mix the two together? I must have missed that memo."

Lana looked at me like I'd lost my mind.

"It's okay," I said. "I'll wait. In the meantime you might not want to step on my toes again. I only have ten of them, and I happen to like them all."

"You need to listen to the music," Lana said. "Your feet should move with the rhythm. You have to feel it, experience it, take it all in." She moved, and I tried to follow her. "You're not even trying."

"Am too," I said.

"Are you a little kid?"

"Sometimes," I said. "Women tell me I have as much energy as one. What do you think?"

She groaned. "Do you listen? You move when the music moves, not before."

"Once in a while," I said.

"Are you hoping to get laid?"

"Always."

"Well, you're not going to have women swooning if you can't master a few simple dance moves," Lana said. "Anyone can do the waltz. You make a box, and you lead with your right foot. The guy always leads. If you make the woman do all the work, you're going to get about as lucky as a fisherman without any bait."

"Do you think you could switch with me?" I asked. "I can be pretty good at following orders. I'll even let you take my clothes off first."

She squeezed my hand tighter. To my credit I didn't wince. "You don't have a choice in the matter. And you may look good, but you don't look that good."

"I could wear a skirt and everything." I laughed, just for the fun of it.

"Guys don't wear skirts; they wear kilts." Lana looked good in her schoolgirl outfit—all she needed was the pigtails and the girlish grin. I tried not to stare. But every once in a while my tongue fell out of my mouth, and I had to push it back in. I wanted to push something else in—it would have gotten me a quick slap in the face.

"I could wear one of those, too." I'd never worn either, and I wouldn't wear one for a million bucks. It was important to keep things in perspective. At the moment, I had a lot of perspective.

"You're not even Scottish," Lana said.

"How would you know?"

"Well, are you?" she asked.

"I'm Irish."

"There ya go."

"But I'm also English, German, Swedish, and Danish." I would've taken a little bow—I didn't think it was a good idea. I had to concentrate rather hard on avoiding toes.

"What kind of heritage is that?"

"I'm a man from many lands," I said.

By the fourth song, my land grab had improved to the conquering stage. Lana and I made it through an entire tune, minus the stepping on toes bit, and I displayed both promise and rhythm—her words not mine.

Learning the waltz wasn't quite as difficult as I thought. After all, it was all about the box.

22

After I learned a few dance moves, I decided it was time to do more research, and the best place to conduct research was the Internet. Since I happened to have a computer in my office, and since it happened to be connected to the Internet, and since it might give me the chance to look at the mysterious Mandy Humphrey a few more times—as well as possibly engage in more stimulating conversation with her—I decided to head back to my office. Maybe she would even sit in one of my two client chairs. That way it would give me a better view of her legs. I needed a good leg shot or two to help me refocus, reinvigorate my case, and help me reach the end of the race.

While I surfed the Internet—not my favorite type of surfing—I refilled my empty coffee cup, stared out across the street at nothing in particular, leaned back in my chair, counted the number of women that I'd slept with, stopping when I reached twenty, even though I could have gone a good deal higher, and waited for Mandy to grace me with her presence.

I wondered what the odds were that she and I might consummate our relationship soon. Since we hadn't even been out on a date, I figured they weren't as good as I'd like for them to be. She had learned a decent enough wink, but I could have done better, and my wink would have caused her to lose her clothes on the spot. That's why I kept my winking to a minimum.

After my brief interlude away from reality, I jerked myself back to the task at hand. The second cup of coffee did the trick, and I'd discovered a few leads. The first murder case had been buried not long after it had surfaced, and I wondered why. However, a few facts did ring true: The case involved a dead dancer named Cindy Bell; apparently, she had died from a drug overdose; the drug of choice was cocaine; her death was ruled a suicide; she had a two paragraph obituary in the newspaper; and she was survived by her boyfriend Clay Dedham and her parents Ty and Evelyn Bell, who now lived on the western side of Richmond in a suburb called Short Pump.

Cindy was an itty-bitty thing with a radiant smile, long, straight, blond hair, exceptionally white teeth, no history of drug use that I'd been able to find, although her boyfriend had used, and her boyfriend passed away three years later in a car accident. He struck a tree at eighty miles an hour, it was a single-car accident, and there were no skid marks leading up to the tree. His death, while suspicious, never did have any more leads. I wanted more.

So I decided to take a drive in my Dodge Viper SRT-10. I could drive with the top down, The Point on the radio, my gelled hair remaining stiff against the breeze, the sun beating down on my face, and two lanes of traffic most of the way, passing cities like Hampton, Newport News, and Williamsburg, as the trees along I-64 saluted me. Traffic was light in the later morning hours, once I reached the other side of the Hampton Roads Bridge Tunnel. And I cranked my Viper up over seventy-five without too much trouble, although I had to whiz past some old ladies and older men on their way to the local bingo parlors.

I called ahead and found Ty Bell to be somewhat accommodating, if not a little suspicious in nature. Suspicion was the name of the game in my world, and I would have been more surprised if he had invited me over with open arms. That's where my charm comes in handy, although it works better with the ladies, and its highest success rate involves getting them to drop their underwear. Since

I wasn't in the mood to see any granny panties, I was glad I had talked to Ty and not Evelyn.

"So you're the young man I spoke with on the phone," Ty said.

"I am, indeed," I said. "I make a much better impression in person."

"Are you some kind of comedian?" Ty asked. He wore pressed slacks, a polo shirt, leather loafers, a bald head, no glasses, and no smile. He stood just over six feet tall. His wife had sculpted gray hair, fashionable lenses, pressed slacks, and a pale blue blouse.

"That depends on your definition of comedian," I said.

"I'm not a fan of Adam Sandler or Jim Carrey," he said.

"I'm not either."

"How can we help you?" Evelyn asked.

"Could you tell me more about your daughter's death?"

"Why the sudden curiosity? She's been dead for fourteen years."

"I know. But I'm investigating another murder at the Virginia Dance Company, and I'm wondering if the two might be related."

He asked, "Did the new girl die of a drug overdose?"

"No."

"Did she have a boyfriend?"

"Yes. And apparently she had a girlfriend as well."

"Kids these days are liable to try just about anything," Ty said. "And I thought the sixties was a crazy time."

Evelyn said, "What makes you think they might be related?"

"I don't know," I said. "At this point, I'm just entertaining theories. It's rather interesting to me that the VDC has now had two dead dancers. In your daughter's case, while it was ruled a suicide, I find it rather convenient."

"We did too, son."

"So your daughter never used drugs before?"

"No," he said. "She was a good kid with a good head on her shoulders, not the best choice in men, but Clay Dedham wasn't a bad kid."

That was Cindy's boyfriend, otherwise known as the drug user.

"Just a bit misdirected at times. He'd promised to clean up his act, and as far as we'd known, he had. That's what made her death so damn frustrating and so hard for us to accept. The police seemed to stop trying before they ever really started."

We were in a living room the size of my first apartment, and while Ty didn't appear to be much of a pacer, he'd been pacing for the past several minutes while we talked about his daughter's death. A girl who, in fact, was their only daughter. I, on the other hand, was more of a sitter and a listener, although there were times when I didn't do either particularly well. For the time being, I happened to be focused on both. They hadn't offered and I hadn't asked for any sort of refreshment.

The sofa was soft, cream-colored leather that felt more than a tad pricey. The paintings on the walls were all originals, and the house was brick, modern, and three stories. I felt right at home, and I could have had a nice nap on the leather. All I needed was a fluffy pillow.

"Are you thinking about our daughter?" Evelyn asked.

"I was thinking about taking a nap on your sofa."

"Have you ever heard of the word restraint?" he asked.

"Maybe you should use it in a sentence."

"Just what kind of detective are you?"

"I'm a PI," I said.

"That's even worse. Are you smart enough to solve both cases?"

"I am."

"Have you ever heard the word modesty?"

"I have. But I don't think it's applicable in this situation." I paused. "So what else can you tell me about your daughter?"

"Well, right before she died, she wasn't happy," Evelyn said.

"Did you ever find out why?"

"I know she and Clay were having some problems, and I know she'd lost some of her enthusiasm for dancing. But she wouldn't tell me why."

"What do you think it might have been?"

Evelyn said, "I think Veronica might have been pushing her too hard."

23

After my trip beyond Richmond and back, I decided to make another trip to my office, and not because I had any notions of seeing Mandy Humphrey naked, although I wouldn't object should such an occurrence take place. However, I figured I had better odds of having sex with four women.

I did more research, and I learned a few new bits of useful information. Clay Dedham had a bit of a gambling problem, not the least of which was that he liked to bet on the now defunct Houston Oilers; he'd been arrested for shoplifting at the age of twenty-three; and he had four speeding tickets to his name, the last of which was written three months before his death. He had two other steady girlfriends that I could find, he'd been a two-sport athlete—basketball and baseball—during which he'd developed his drug problem; and he'd been clean for the last four years of his life.

Since I felt in a parenting mood, and since I hadn't called on Jessica's parents, Frank and Jill Mason, recently, I figured it was high time I paid them a visit. If their personalities were anything like the last time I'd visited them, I was in for a real treat.

"What the heck are you doing here?" Frank asked.

"I was in a visiting mood."

"I hope you're not staying for dinner," he said.

Dinner was still several hours away, at least by my watch, although older people did tend to eat earlier in the day. Either way, I wasn't in the mood for pork chops, or whatever the choice meal of the day happened to be.

"No, I'll be well on my way before then. I just have a few questions."

"Well, come on in," Jill said. "Don't mind Frank. He hasn't had his afternoon pills yet."

Since every older person I knew took some sort of medication—blood pressure pills, cholesterol tablets, heart medication, Viagra, arthritis pills, or gout tablets—I wasn't shocked by the revelation. I would have been more shocked had Jill told me Frank could still get it up three times a day without any help from the little blue pills. And if said conversation had taken place, I would have decided on an early exit strategy.

As I stepped through the threshold, the smell of fresh apple pie filled my nostrils.

I asked, "Did you know there was a previous death at Virginia Dance Company?"

"Are you talking about Cindy Bell?" Frank asked.

"Good. So you do know about it."

"Just what are you getting at, buster?"

"Most of the time I have no idea. In this case, I'm trying to figure out if there might be any link between the two. At this point, I'm just grasping at straws."

"In your case, you must have a pretty long straw, because her death was ruled a suicide."

"Exactly," I said. "I've always been known to reach for the ceiling with my feet firmly planted on the ground." I shifted on the sofa. It was still as uncomfortable as the last time I was here. The imitation art still tried to imitate, and two sets of eyes stared at me with intense curiosity. "Just because her death was ruled a suicide, doesn't necessarily mean the cops reached the right conclusion. Officers have been known to make mistakes, especially when they're overworked, underpaid, and eat doughnuts three times a day."

He said, "You don't appear as though you downed too many doughnuts; your hair resembles those male models I see on TV; and I'd bet my next Social Security check that Viper out in my driveway isn't leased."

"Wow," I said. "Nothing gets past you. Maybe I should take you along with me. You could be the new Mini-Me." I didn't bother to point out that he was still a good five years away from his first Social Security check. It would have spoiled my Mini-Me line, and I didn't want to appear more of a smartass than I already was.

"You'd have to change shirts first. I'm not riding around with someone who's got humping bunnies front and center surrounded by a pale blue background."

"It brings out the white and gray bunnies," I said.

"I'm sure it does."

"Did either of you hear of any unusual circumstances surrounding Cindy's death?"

"You mean like the fact that she didn't use drugs?" Jill asked.

"Exactly," I said. "See, we're already getting somewhere."

When I asked how she happened to be so smart, Jill told me she had taught Cindy Bell in high school—she had been an English teacher—and she just happened to be the nicest, sweetest, straight-A student this side of the Appalachian mountains.

I told her that was quite an accomplishment, and Jill flashed me a sweet smile.

"What else can you tell me about her?" I said.

"Her taste in boys could have used a bit of tweaking. She always fell for the bad ones who were the star athletes and had trouble even spelling calculus."

"Every young girl's fantasy."

Frank asked, "What sport did you play, Casey?"

"I was a football player. I played free safety before I blew out my knee in college. Now I just stick to running and surfing."

"And for some strange reason you still manage to break women's hearts," Frank said. "I bet you have no idea why."

I smiled. "It's because of my charm."

"It's because of your confidence and persistence."

"I don't have to persistently chase women."

"No, Casey, you don't. But some day when your looks fade, and you're old and gray, you just might wish you had."

Since I didn't want to tell him he was full of crap and that would never happen, I just nodded. The sofa became even more uncomfortable as the plastic crinkled beneath my bottom, and I noticed more than two pairs of eyes staring back at me.

"Do you have any leads in our daughter's case?" Jill asked.

"Not exactly. I have a lot of suspects, some who I like more than others, none of whom appear to have revealed their true selves to me yet."

"For a smart guy," he said, "you almost sound like a politician."

"I take it you're not a fan."

"I hate politicians. Ever since Ronald Reagan we've had nothing but nut cases in the White House, and as far as I could tell, Ronald probably had a few screws loose himself. What we need is a president with some balls who's not afraid to take action."

"Isn't that an oxymoron?"

Before he could answer, Jill handed Frank two or three pills, all of which were white, and he downed them all with a glass of orange juice.

"You know, for a guy who wears obscene t-shirts and uses too much gel in his hair, you're not half bad."

I gave him one of my best grins.

"So who do you think killed my daughter?"

I noticed he didn't use *our*.

"Well, I've narrowed it down to someone in the VDC, ever since I punched Derrick Stevens in the jaw and he didn't squeal like a pig, but I just don't know which dancer, or executive, actually committed the crime. That place has more problems than our current Senate."

"Well, when you do find out who it is, I want first dibs on breaking his legs."

I noticed he didn't use the word *she.*

24

"Have you come to clean my pipes?" Gloria Headwitz asked, as she hung on her front door.

"Well, if you need me to, I'm going to need a longer pole."

"I think your pole will do just fine."

Along with some new information for my case, Ty and Evelyn Bell had given me the names of Cindy's former friends who were still in the area. Since I didn't have an unlimited budget, being that Kathryn Gable was my backer, I decided to cut costs where I could. That'd mean my visits to the strip club would no longer be an issue. Not that there were any before, but if there had been, they would have been the first extraneous expense to go. Paying to view breasts was a foreign concept for me.

"My pole probably shouldn't come out to play," I said. "He's been a bit oversexed the past few days, and I think he's better off staying hidden. That way he doesn't poke where he doesn't belong."

"Suit yourself," she said. "So what do you want, since I can't talk you out of your clothes? You might as well come inside. I won't bite unless provoked."

It was a tempting offer, I had to admit. While she was in her forties—she looked like a yoga or Pilates gal—she could have just as easily passed for her thirties. She had a crooked tooth, just off center, a small mole on her left cheek, and a sultry, sexy voice.

I sat; she stood. She started to rub my shoulders; I inched away. I asked her to sit; she did so after some initial reluctance.

"So how'd you get the voice?"

"I'm a former nightclub singer. Now, I work a phone sex line."

I couldn't think of a smart comeback to that one, so I just kept my mouth shut.

"Well, you certainly have the voice for it. You have the voice of someone in her twenties. If I heard you on the other end of the line, I'd think Playboy model."

"Well," she said, "aren't you the little charmer?"

"I am, ma'am."

"If you call me ma'am one more time, I'm going to cut off your balls."

I happened to like my balls, so I didn't call her ma'am again. "So what can you tell me about Cindy Bell?"

She gave me a long, hard look after my abrupt topic shift. "She died fourteen years ago. You're a bit late to the party, governor."

"I'm always a bit behind the times." I wasn't, but it sounded appropriate, and I'd rather have women underestimate me than overestimate me. "Her parents said you knew her well."

"I did. She and I were best friends—up until the day she died. I didn't have the talent to dance, but she could walk on water, as far as I was concerned. Her boyfriend, the sleaze bag, thought so too."

The sleaze bag was none other than Clay Dedham.

"He was better at using women than he was about sustaining relationships."

There were people who said the same thing about me.

"But she loved him, never did stop loving him, and it's probably what killed her."

"Do you think he did it?"

"No, it seemed a bit too convenient for me. He'd even stopped using drugs. She'd threatened to leave him if he didn't. I don't think she would have actually done it, her heart was too big, and she was in it too deep—we're talking six feet over her head deep—but he cared enough about her to actually change, when he wasn't trying to get busy with the next cute piece of tail."

Another one of my faults.

"She told me he was hung like a garden hose. Had to have been, otherwise he wouldn't have been able to keep the women, because he certainly didn't have much going on between his ears."

"So you think he might have had something to do with her death?"

"Not personally. No way. He'd never hit anything in his life that wasn't inanimate. But his actions caused her death. What I mean by that is someone probably—"

"Killed her to get to him, or killed her because of him."

"Exactly. Smart, sexy, not an ounce of fat on you, and blond. I could make your eyes pop out of their sockets, your toes curl, and you'd lick the back of your throat with your tongue."

I had no doubt that she could, and if I had any less willpower, I would have taken her up on her offer. Her breasts were real, still winners, and she knew how to use them. And she used just the right inflection in her voice, lingering over the important words, the ones that could knock your socks off. Luckily, mine stayed on.

"I'll bet you do Pilates," I said.

"Pilates, yoga—and I could do you. I can go for hours, days even."

Again, I didn't have a doubt in my mind. If I didn't get out of her house in the next hour, I had a vision that she'd tie me up with nylon rope, shred my clothes with her fingernails, and ride me until I had a heart attack. Since I was in the best shape of my life, that was a hard concept for me to follow.

"Did Clay have any mob ties?"

"Why would you ask a question like that?"

"I'm just throwing watermelons at the wall, trying to get one of them to burst." Since the mob loaned out money to unscrupulous individuals, and in some cases, the mob had ties to the gambling arena, it wasn't a huge stretch for me. Clay was a sports jock.

"Well," she said, "that's a very good guess, and I'd have to say you're one hundred percent correct. Funny, the cops never put that scenario together."

"Not that you know of, anyway," I said.

"Touché. May I get you a drink?"

"No, thanks. I don't drink on the job." Well, sometimes I did, but I didn't want Gloria to get me drunk. I might end up tied to her bed without my clothes.

While she headed for the kitchen, I took in her living room with a bit more scrutiny. I'd seen the pictures of her that covered the walls; I'd noticed the plush carpeting, the two full length mirrors and the one on the ceiling, the swinging chandelier, and the pair of pink panties poking out of the sofa. I wasn't the first young stud Gloria had tried to talk out of his clothes, and I knew I wouldn't be the last. It wasn't a blow to my ego, since my ego didn't take potshots, but it did help me keep things in perspective.

"So he had a bit of a gambling problem?"

"Problem isn't a strong enough word. It was more like an epidemic. During football season, Clay had a standing account with the local bookie. He'd bet on four games every Sunday, and he'd lose three of them."

"Maybe he should have stuck to coloring books," I said.

She stuffed some of the multi-colored drink in her mouth. I watched her stuff it, lick her lips, and then go for more. If she lost any more of her inhibitions she was going to walk around without a stitch on her, and I'd have myself a prime viewing. All I needed was a video camera, which might've been hidden behind one of the full-length mirrors, since I had the distinct impression hers weren't the only set of eyes watching me.

"What else can you tell me about their relationship?"

"Cindy wanted to get pregnant, she was ready for the challenge, always wanted to have a few young ones running around the house, and she thought Clay would make a decent enough father, since he'd gotten himself reformed and all. I told her she should look at this a bit more rationally, but once Cindy got an idea in her head, there was no way anyone could get it back out again. Of course, Veronica wasn't real keen on the idea."

"I heard the two of them had a falling out."

"Exactly," Gloria said. She downed the rest of her glass. Her eyes took on a transparent, more lucid quality.

"And it was over the pregnancy?"

"Not necessarily, but it certainly didn't help the cause. Cindy wanted to leave the Virginia Dance Company to start a family, hoped Clay might find himself a real job—he had a few prospects going, as he liked to say—and they planned on starting their new life together."

"Only she was killed before said plan could be implemented."

25

I drove over to the Virginia Dance Company, feeling a little light-headed, a little out of my league, and as though my whole life were a movie played out for me to see. There I was, tied to a chair, with my eyes held open using toothpicks. It wasn't what I'd call a pleasant experience. So far, most of the case hadn't been what I'd refer to as pleasant, although it did have a few moments here and there.

Traffic had picked up, the rain had started falling, and my top was up. I didn't have a bottom to put down, otherwise I would have, and I would have plugged myself right in. The engine revved, and my mind raced, mostly with unpleasant thoughts, misguided notions, and naked women championing my cause. I needed a little more action and a lot more sex for me to feel truly at ease.

I arrived at the VDC minus the screeching tires and grand entrance, although peeling into the parking lot did hold a certain appeal. I passed a few dancers on my way to see Veronica Sutton, some I had talked to and one or two I hadn't, but I couldn't spread myself too thin; otherwise, I might not make it across both slices of bread, and I happened to have a rather large appetite. I figured it was all the talk about sex and my ability to show a little restraint. But I turned my focus directly to the cause: Veronica's office.

She sat at her desk, bent slightly forward, staring at a computer screen with raised eyebrows and a hard expression.

I coughed.

She looked up and her expression turned even darker.

I smiled.

It didn't work.

Rather than waste time, I dove right into the deep end. "You didn't tell me a dancer died fourteen years ago," I said.

"Aren't you going to start with a 'Nice to see you'? Or at least maybe, 'Hello'?" Veronica said. She had on a little less makeup, a smirk on her face, papers piled over an inch high on the right hand corner of her desk, one or two prominent photos stuck out front and center, along with paintings of dancers behind her and on either side of her, and her hair was styled to perfection.

"That was a long time ago," she added.

"I'm getting that a lot lately. However, I happen to think it's relevant information."

"It was a suicide," Veronica said.

"It was never investigated properly."

"It was an open-and-shut case."

"Once in a while those open-and-shut cases involve people hiding information they don't want to get out," I said. "And that's when my mind kicks into overdrive." My mind had only one speed, and it wasn't hanging out in the slow lane.

"Your mind is always in overdrive. You might want to shift it down to neutral once in a while. You might save yourself an ulcer by the time you hit forty."

I was a hair over thirty, so forty was a long way off. "There are a lot of gears between overdrive and neutral."

"And you seem to miss them all," she said.

The computer keys tapped, papers shuffled, and I still stood. Her office may have been slightly bigger than mine, but I had a better desk and chair. In fact, if a fire burned my office to the ground, I wanted to ensure I saved my desk and chair, myself—and

Mandy Humphrey. The rest of it could burn.

"I also heard you and Cindy had a falling out," I said.

"So, you found out her name?" she said. "Well, good for you. I can get you a cookie to go with your glass of milk."

There was no glass of milk, so I didn't expect a cookie to magically appear either. Veronica Sutton had nothing on David Copperfield.

"I'm conducting an investigation."

"At someone else's expense. And you don't even seem to be doing a good job of it. You are creating a major headache for my dancers, as well as me, and we have a performance in less than two weeks. If our show doesn't go off on schedule, the VDC could see red. And to top it all off, you are stirring up the past instead of focusing on the present. You aren't going to find any new information on Cindy Bell's suicide, so you should give it up. The cops knew what they were doing."

There were two problems with her previous comments. First, people only tell you not to pursue a logical angle if they have something to hide. Second, even cops make mistakes, and it didn't take me a few years of wearing the uniform for me to figure that one out.

"Once in a while the two happen to be related," I said. "It's like putting down concrete: You have to start at one end to get to the other, and you have to work around any obstacles that happen to show up."

"Are you dropping tangerines from the sky? If you are, maybe you need to open your mouth a little wider."

"Maybe I am," I said. "Why don't you give me some straight answers?"

Her right eye twitched—her tell. "What do you want to know?"

"What did you and Cindy fight about?"

"She wanted to have a baby, and I told her it was a ridiculous concept to entertain. Her boyfriend was a loser, she was at the top of her game, and we had a scheduled performance in just over a month. You don not mess with a deadline."

Where have I heard that one before? I said, "You could always hire a replacement."

She scoffed. "You don't hire a replacement for one of the best dancers in your company. You find a way to keep her around."

What did keeping her around involve? "And did you?"

"I was working on it," Veronica said. "Someone needed to talk some sense into that girl. She had her legs wrapped around unreality."

"I heard she was rather stubborn when she put her mind to something."

"We could say the same thing about someone else in this room."

I didn't think she was talking about herself. Since Veronica and I had made zero headway on Cindy's death, I decided to transition to the current dead one: Jessica Mason. "Jessica was pregnant, almost a month along. That's enough time to notify your lover, your friends, a colleague—or your boss."

"I know. She did notify me."

At least she didn't try to deny it like she had the last time.

"Don't you find that just a bit convenient? She told you about something intensely personal in her life, and now she's dead."

"Convenient for whom? You or your case? If you're looking for a killer, you are looking in the wrong place. I take very good care of my dancers."

"Right now," I said, "they're related." I meant being pregnant and being dead.

"Only because you can't separate yourself from the task at hand. You can't boil everything in one pot and expect it to come out perfect."

I stretched my toes, and then reached for the ceiling. "Who was the father?"

"I have no idea."

"That worked last time," I said. "But it's not going to work again."

"Bradley Cassidy."

26

"What the hell do you want?" Derrick Stevens said. His eyes blazed, his breathing came in short spurts, and he stared at me the way you might watch a person on death row die.

"You already used that line the last time."

"I've already called the cops," he said.

He hadn't used that line the last time. "Well, you might want to call them off. You and I have a few things we need to talk about."

"I have nothing to say to you." He tried to forcefully slam the door, but to no avail. He didn't work out the way I did. Most people didn't. It was easier to be lazy.

"Well, I have a few things to say to you. And I hope I can get it all done before the cops break up our little party."

"They're fast."

I knew he was lying. I'd seen Stephens and Mayberry in action, and they were anything but fast. However, Ian was a full step ahead of the rest of the gang; I had friends in high places. It often served me well.

"Then, I'll be faster," I said. "Did you know Jessica liked to get around?"

"Don't talk about her that way."

I had his attention.

The gaze remained, and it had a renewed focus.

"Apparently, she had a couple lovers other than you, of the male *and* female variety, and the other male happened to plant his seed inside her."

I watched; I waited; I held the door; and then I snapped my fingers.

"You mean she was pregnant?"

I took a little bow.

"But she never told me . . ."

"And why would she?" I said. "It wasn't yours."

He tried to punch me, *tried* being the operative word. I grabbed his fist in midair, held it there for a three count, and then I squeezed, while he let out a little squeal.

"Maybe you should work on being less crude," he said.

"Maybe you should work on keeping your hands to yourself," I said. "If you can't play nice, I'll take your tongue and wrap it around your head. And then I'll make you swallow it."

"You're an animal."

"I've been called a lot worse." I'd been called a thug, a thief, a liar, and a cheat. None of which came even remotely close to describing my actual personality.

"Are you going to drop any more bombshells in my lap? Or are we done for the day? I can get this kind of abuse from an ex-girlfriend." Derrick still had one hand on the door, just in case I decided to let go.

"Did you know one of the VDC's dancers committed suicide fourteen years ago?"

"I heard something about it," he said.

"What do you remember?"

"Why do you care?" Derrick asked.

The hostility, while hidden at times, had never really gone away. And I thought my charm had started to do me some good.

"I like to tie up all loose ends."

"You can tie them up somewhere else." Derrick stuck his fist in my direction, and again, I caught it in midair. Only this time I leveled him to the ground.

And that was when the cops showed up.

"I think we're looking at an assault charge," Mayberry said, "aren't we, Rick?"

Stephens, who never really had much of a comment, said nothing.

"Officer, this man is a menace to society," Derrick said.

"He's more like a stop sign: He keeps showing up where we don't want him to. And then he tries to gun his engine."

"I only know one word," I said, "and that's *go*."

I now had three short, stocky men to deal with, all with quick tempers, no personality, and no sense of humor. It was the relationship equivalent of meeting three ex-girlfriends at the same time. And not exactly the women of my dreams.

However, I did have one woman who remained in my dreams, for different reasons, and I figured it was about time to pay her a visit. With the cops gone, the situation was resolved: It involved a heated, nonviolent discussion during which time I told the whole truth and nothing but the truth; my mouth had other uses besides those of a sexual nature.

My head was once again filled with newfound information, and there was no end to the case in sight. I decided it was time for a little perspective. I'd need a lot if I was ever going to get out of this case alive.

Dragon Lady had a free moment, and I happened to be a free man, so it worked to both of our advantages. As I made my grand entrance, I scanned the cavernous room with hardwood floors clean enough for me to see my reflection, the pristine dance floor, and I noticed a musty smell in the air, with the faint hint of cigarette smoke.

The bar was clean and empty, the glasses were empty and lined up on the bar, and I had snuck in through the back door. I grabbed a stool, tapped the counter, and waited for her undivided attention.

It didn't happen, but I did watch her clean a couple of glasses, hum a few bars of some foreign tune, and juggle three mugs at once.

"Why is it women in a position of authority always lash out at men?"

She shook her head. "Not all women do."

"So you're saying I get special abuse?"

"No, I'm saying not all women are created equal." She cleaned a glass with a white towel. Her t-shirt sparkled white, her hair was shorter than mine, and the L-shaped bar was clean enough for me to lick it.

"We're more different than you realize. You can't put us all in the same bikini and toss us in the same swimming pool."

I had no idea how she knew I was thinking about bikinis at that particular moment. I didn't bother to ask; life was too short to worry about the minor details: I had a hard enough time with the major ones.

"I find that hard to believe."

"That doesn't surprise me," Dragon Lady said.

"Does anything surprise you?"

"With you," she said, "not much. With others, maybe once in a while. Your life is filled with clichés and hidden innuendoes. You haven't even stepped onto a reasonable playing surface, and you're already going for the end zone. Your drive often takes you in the wrong direction—"

"Then why do you continue to help me?"

"Are you going to keep your Viper?"

"I am," I said. "I'd throw myself off a cliff before I ever stopped driving a Viper. In fact, if they ever stop making them, I'll figure out a way to restore them myself, or I'll find a man who can do it for me. If someone ever hits me, I'll get out of the car and beat the snot out of him."

"What if he turns out to be a she?"

I had a feeling her question had multiple meanings, but I didn't have multiple answers. "I don't discriminate when it comes to my Viper."

"Then I won't discriminate against you, either," she said. "Life isn't about trying to change people or make everyone the same, it's about accepting people's differences and learning to live with them.

Besides, you need help on a fairly regular basis. Your ability to find trouble is off the charts. And once in a while you actually have something intelligent to say. However, when it comes to women, you're about as clueless as a blind dog with no nose. You try hard, though, and you mean well. If you can learn to keep your mouth in check, your world will be filled with endless possibilities."

I don't want endless possibilities, I want women in bikinis.

"My mouth happens to be good for a lot of things. And there's no way I could ever keep it in check."

Dragon Lady finished her line of glasses and put them away. Each one had a specific location, and each one gave me a very specific view of her bottom.

"The most frequent thing it's good for is getting you in trouble," she said. "You need to learn when to tone it down. And you should be required to obtain a license to operate your eyes. You're staring at me with the hormonal response of a teenager."

"You know, Ian is always telling me the exact same thing. The eye comment, however, is a new one."

"Plus, there's your other little problem: You don't listen to him, either."

"How do you know?" I said. I didn't like having my mind read. I preferred to keep my rather random thoughts to myself, that way I could keep myself out of trouble—occasionally. Otherwise, I'd have trouble nailed down pat.

"You always ask questions, and I always have the answers. Haven't we already established the boundaries of this relationship? You can't go back and change the rules in the middle of the game. You'd never get out alive."

"Yes," I said, "but it doesn't hurt to have constant reinforcement."

The glasses were all put away, and now we were in the middle of a staring contest. I had plenty of time to assess my opponent, and this is one battle that I knew, no matter how hard I tried or what rules I decided to break, there was no way I could win. I was out matched, but I wasn't going to be outclassed.

"Some need more reinforcement than most," she said. "You, however, fall somewhere in the middle. Your stubbornness is legendary, but without it, you wouldn't stand a chance."

A few stragglers had started to trickle in. Most of them weren't blond or women; therefore, I wasn't interested. Dragon Lady had started lining up beers, Jack Daniels, and mixed drinks. In one smooth motion she sent them sailing toward the end of the bar in either direction. My seat in the middle had yet to be invaded, and I wanted to keep it that way.

While she kept the drinks flowing, I punched a few keys on the jukebox and had Bruce Springsteen and Foreigner lined up and ready for action. As far as thinking-music went, that was about as good as it got for me.

"Can I talk to you about the case?" I asked.

She winked at me. "What else are we going to talk about?"

"In my pursuit of solving the first case, I happened upon a suicide by one of the VDC's dancers fourteen years ago."

"But you don't think it's a suicide?"

"Let's put it this way, I'm not completely convinced. The case could have been mishandled, since the evidence proved a suicide, and in their haste to wrap up a case the detectives may have missed a few details. It's easy to go with the information given and to forget any and all other leads. Even the best cops make mistakes from time to time."

"This sounds like an area you're familiar with," Dragon Lady said.

"I'm not too proud to admit I've made my share of mistakes. I just try not to repeat the same ones. Otherwise, I'll end up in the hack department."

She filled a mug to the brim, letting a little foam spill over the side. "If it was a cover-up, the obvious question is: What did the killer, or the cops, want to hide."

"Well," I said, "Cindy Bell—that's the first victim—did want to get pregnant with her flawed boyfriend, and she had talked about leaving the VDC. As for victim number two, Jessica Mason, she was a month along, and so far, the only one who knew about her pregnancy was Veronica Sutton. And the first time I talked to her, she lied. But she isn't the first person who lied to me, and she won't be the last."

"Love hides many flaws. Who's the father?"

"Well, Derrick Stevens wasn't, Kathryn Gable couldn't have impregnated her, so that leaves Bradley Cassidy, the other man in her life. According to Veronica Sutton, he's the father. I haven't had a chance to speak with him again, to get his side of the story, but if he didn't want the kid or Jessica and he disagreed on the raising of their child, that would create enough motivation for murder. Or he might have been a sperm donor and nothing more."

"But that doesn't rule out Derrick Stevens or Kathryn Gable, either," she said. "Jilted lovers will go to the ends of the earth to even the score."

"True," I said. "Derrick's DNA doesn't check out on Jessica's body, and Bradley did end up with a new watch not long after Jessica's death. However, Bradley is an easy target, since he's the father. He's a dancer at the VDC, and he's strong enough to move a dead body. If he can lift women up by the buttocks with one hand, he could move a limp, dead dancer. Are you trying to ensure I view all angles?"

"I'm just trying to change your perspective a bit," Dragon Lady said. "You, like most men, often have no clue what you're up against. Even when you think things through, you often miss the obvious."

27

Dragon Lady and I finished up, and I dodged her advances to drive my Viper. With customers around it wasn't hard to talk her out of her position, and I decided I was in the mood for some action after all. I had my gun shoved down the front of my pants to prove it. But I wanted to hit the seas instead of the open road. With my last dance lesson mastered—I'd discovered my ability to make a box—I knew I needed another lesson from my teacher to truly cement my talent.

I called Lana Ralstein, the dancer with more attitude than sense and my previous dance instructor, on her cell phone, told her I had commandeered a vessel, and asked her if she wanted to be my first mate. When she said yes, I scrambled to find a boat. Money can buy you anything, and I had a few Benjamin Franklins lying around for just such an emergency.

The boat was white, as shiny as a bottle cap glistening in the sun. It had a black racing stripe along the side, enough room to seat eight comfortably, a two-tiered deck, and a large sail decorated with a golf bag. Its name was *Big Bertha*. I'd never been much of a golfer, but the name wasn't lost on me.

Lana's body glistened, the string bikini had small strings strategically placed with the fabric, and her hair fell just past her shoulders. She had met me on the dock with her thumb pointed toward the sky, a sly grin on her face and just enough fabric to constitute a toddler's outfit—not that I was complaining.

After I helped Lana onboard, I tossed my gun below deck.

I was glad I had something else to concentrate on aside from her. The boat proved even more challenging than I had anticipated; technically, I didn't have a license to operate watercraft. String bikinis and perfect bottoms only heightened my senses on the open water.

As if she could read my mind, she demanded to know where I had currently placed my attention, right before she bent over at the waist and began fishing around in her beach bag.

"If we get into the gory details of what's going through my head, I have a feeling I'll be one person short of a good time."

I looked around. The open water didn't hold nearly the opportunities Lana offered, and I was sure I hadn't even gotten to all the good ones yet. My outfit consisted of my best pair of American Eagle trunks. I made sure they had Eagle written across the butt. I figured it was important to have every woman I came in contact with read my behind. So far it hadn't worked with Lana. It would have helped my cause if I had my bottom pointed in her direction—like she had done with me—however, she'd have to put on the captain's hat and commandeer my vessel, and I wasn't sure I was ready for that level of commitment.

I paid off the boat's normal caretakers to ensure we weren't disturbed for the evening and had rented the boat through the night; I brought takeout, just in case Lana was the kind of woman who could blow up a kitchen with her mind; and even though the owner was a friend of a friend, I was still out more Benjamin Franklins than my PI budget allowed. It helped to have reserves for such sexual emergencies.

I wanted Lana to moon me, though I was pretty sure she wouldn't. She hadn't even bent over—other than the one time. The view was intoxicating—it almost steered me off course—and it was more than I had bargained for, especially considering my current depletion of funds. I pondered how the small bit of fabric held everything in place. I couldn't think of a single good answer, so I continued to stare, just in case I happened to come up with any bright ideas. On a positive note, her ass helped me forget about the two cases I had yet to solve. There were dollar bills everywhere, if you knew where to look.

"What do you think holds that bikini together?" I asked. "I know it's not gravity." Her breasts pushed the thin fabric to its maximum, and I had to keep the lower half of my body in check. I had a few ideas. I decided not to mention them; otherwise, I might get thrown overboard, and I wasn't wearing a life jacket.

She smiled, then she bent over at the waist to pick up an imaginary quarter. "I'm not too sure. What do you think it is?"

I coughed. "You don't seem like the indecisive type. You always know exactly what you want, and you're not afraid to go after it." I had just described myself to a T, even if I didn't have on the t-shirt to back up my analysis.

The smile out of the side of her mouth was back. "I'm sure you're a man who always knows what he wants. And I know you'll go to great lengths to pursue it."

"I am," I said. "And I do. I'll let you know when I figure out what I need to pursue next. But until then you and I can have a bit of fun."

I noticed a small birthmark in the shape of a heart about six inches from her ass. I'd seen the same birthmark on Jessica Mason's back.

She said, "What did you have in mind?"

"I've never had a woman cook for me naked on my boat."

"It's not your boat."

"It is until I turn it back in," I said. "Don't you think that's better? To take what you want, use it, and then discard it when you're through?" My relationships tended to work out that way. If I wasn't careful, it would probably happen again. "Why should the victor get to keep the spoils?"

"I don't think we're talking about boats anymore."

We weren't. Business and pleasure happened to intertwine on a regular basis.

"Do you sail?" I asked.

"Not usually, no. I'm trying to cut back. If I'm not careful, I'm told I could get skin cancer." She appeared to have spent a bit of time in a tanning bed, and there was one foolproof way to double check. "And I'm not sure I can part with my skin."

If I were her, I wouldn't part with my skin, either.

I heard the wind blow, the engine rumble, and the sound of her breathing; otherwise it was quiet. I had the company of a beautiful woman to keep me in check, and I had an ocean with a slight rock to it to keep me focused.

"What can you part with?" I asked.

She smiled but didn't answer.

I shook my head, and since I didn't have anywhere else to place my hands, I gripped the steering wheel harder. I'd taken a crash course in sailing, and I didn't pass with flying colors, but money bought a lot of privileges, and I had a few extra dollars to spare.

The first time I took a boat out I almost crashed into a harbor, and soon after I headed straight for another boat before I got the steering under control. It wasn't much different than driving a car; however, I didn't properly account for the wake of other boats, the rocky ocean, or the distractions of the sea. There was also another obvious problem: I liked to go full throttle.

Lucky for me, there were no other boats on the water this evening.

I wanted to impress Lana and show her a good time. I wasn't sure she bit on my fishing expedition theory. She'd laughed when I told her all women wear bikinis when they fish, and she'd told me I was incorrigible when she asked where my pole was and I looked between my legs. But she didn't dive off the boat into the water and swim for shore. That, in and of itself, was a valuable accomplishment on my part.

She put her hands in her hair and swayed her hips to some imaginary tune, and the boat veered hard to the left. I concentrated on the quadratic equation.

"You know," she said, "you're making progress in your dance, but you still have a ways to go. I suggest several more sessions, at a minimum. Now if you're interested in being good . . . "

I knew what that meant. I wasn't feeling frisky enough to respond. On second thought I decided it might be a good idea to change my mind. I winked. "I like being good. It gives me more opportunities to be bad later."

She had snuck up behind me, and I could feel her breath on my neck. Her hands rested on my shoulders. "How good?" Lana asked.

"You have no idea," I said.

"I want an estimate of your true talents, and I'm not settling for anything less than your best," she said. Lana dragged me away from the wheel before I could utter any sort of protest. "I've settled before, and I'm not settling again."

I brushed past her, eased back on the throttle, and dropped anchor. I couldn't drop her bikini, otherwise I would have had her ass up in the pale moonlight. So I figured I'd drop something else instead. It kept my mind occupied on other matters.

"You're getting weirder by the minute," I said. "If you grow three heads, I'm tossing you off the boat. I don't care if you're as sexy as lace underwear. There are certain lines a man doesn't cross."

She could have said, "I'm worth it." But she didn't. There were a lot of things she didn't do, but I could count on her, she had taught me some new moves, and she was more available than Christmas Jones.

I slapped her on the bottom, and to her credit, she didn't slap me across the face. She did reach out to grasp my right hand. Her hands were soft, smooth, delicate, manicured, and a little rough around the edges.

We danced against the backdrop of night and cabin lights. I stepped on her toes twice, and she didn't wince once. She offered pointers; I listened. She glided; I shuffled. The deck moved beneath our feet; my hands moved higher; and she let them stay there. My tongue found her mouth; her tongue found mine.

Then the music in my head stopped.

The night cruise would be over before dawn, or I'd owe some serious money in overtime costs. I didn't think the owner would be particularly thrilled either. He was a client—the man knew how to cut deals—and he might decide to start taking his business elsewhere. I couldn't afford to lose him—he got in as much trouble as I did, and he needed help getting out—or I might have to cut back on my vacation time.

"So do you always stop what you start?" she asked.

I didn't make a habit of it.

"What are you talking about?"

"You're preoccupied."

"I'm not allowed to focus my attention elsewhere?" I said. I'd gotten pretty good at blowing off questions, but women always seemed to come up with more. They had a never-ending well from which they drew. I, on the other hand, had more limited resources.

"You are, but I can think of better things I would like to do," she said.

"Such as?" I could play dumb with the best of them, and I felt this was a good opportunity to do so. I didn't know when the opportunity would present itself again. Next time it might not be with a beautiful woman wearing half an outfit.

"I wasn't aware you needed any hints."

I nodded.

"All of a sudden you have no idea what I'm talking about?" she said. "I don't believe it." She paused. "Not even for a second. You always know more than you let on."

Lana had a good point. I'd have to reevaluate it later. At the moment I didn't have a clear head. The light mist had started messing with my brain.

"I like you," I said. "But you're not coming clean with me. You have a lot of secrets. The more I delve into Jessica's death the more complicated it becomes."

"How clean do you want me to be? You can wash me if you'd prefer."

I thought she might remove her top—she didn't.

"I can't do my job unless I know all the details. And there're still a few left waiting to be snagged."

Lana said, "We're a big family."

Just then the quiet waters turned up the volume. I looked around. I couldn't see anything—the additional lighting didn't help much, other than my view of Lana.

Lana hugged herself tightly, and I assumed it was from the cold.

I listened—I didn't hear anything out of the ordinary, even though Lana had turned away from me and looked out to the open water, fear in her eyes.

I couldn't place the fear. My t-shirt read, MAKE A BIG SPLASH. Now it seemed even more appropriate.

I hadn't heard the roar of a boat until now, and I couldn't see two feet beyond our boat because of the dark sky and the thick fog. It had crept in like it had been there the whole time, and I'd missed it. I still couldn't see the other boat: I sensed it.

Less than an hour ago, Lana and I had danced cheek to cheek, and now she didn't want to have anything to do with me. In less than two minutes she'd backed up more than ten steps away from me, and if she backed up much farther, she'd end up going for a swim. On the other hand, she did have her bikini.

Lana began to rock back and forth on her heels, and that's when I went below for my gun. I'd carried it on the boat with me—I don't know why—and I had the feeling I'd need it now. The way Lana acted, it wasn't the Coast Guard coming to do a friendly check on our vessel.

When I popped my head back up, I heard Lana scream. I clicked the safety off, checked around me, and then made my way to where I'd heard the scream only moments ago. Only there was no one there. I crept toward the front of the boat, and that's when I was clocked on the back of my head.

I dropped like a nickel from the top of the Empire State Building.

And the darkness swept over me.

28

I came to at the bottom of the ocean with a chain wrapped around my leg. I wasn't sure how long I'd been out. It couldn't have been very long—I was still alive, but I was running out of oxygen. I deduced—I didn't know for sure—that there had been a delay between being clocked over the head and being shoved over the edge. I remembered the part about the clocking, but not the shoving or the sinking, and the lapse in judgment helped me work through a few things—my problems always managed to get worse before they got better.

I had a good feeling the person who clocked me over the head wanted me to come to in the water, so I could see my own death as it unfolded before my eyes. I didn't suck in water—I could hold my breath for almost two minutes—that only made the end come quicker; instead, I tried to lift my leg. I couldn't. I tried to swim toward the surface, fighting against the tide, my own lack of strength, and the thought of death. My arms and legs weren't powerful enough to break free. I was a strong swimmer with a strong lung capacity, so I knew I had a bigger issue to resolve. And, if all that weren't enough, I couldn't see.

I wiggled around like I was giving the ocean a lap dance—the ocean wasn't biting—and I knew I'd tire out way too quickly if I kept it up. I could feel a scream forming in my throat, and I did my best to head it off before it cut itself loose, before I gasped my last breath and sucked in water instead of air. I didn't need my lungs filling up with water: It was a slow, painful process. Drowning was the worst way to die.

I hoped my gun had gotten knocked over the side with me. I'd bought one of the best models available, and if I was going to lose it wasn't going to be from a lack of trying. However, even the best models wouldn't fire under water. Through water, yes; under water, no. I felt around, blindly, and I grasped something hard and big—it wasn't my gun. It had a rough surface, and it just might break the binds that held me. I lifted it with both hands and slammed it against the shackle. I wiggled my leg—it was still bound—so I slammed the object against the chain once more. I didn't feel anything move this time either: My leg still wasn't free. I was running on empty, but I still had a few fumes left in me, and I decided to make each one of them count. What I didn't count on was water filling my lungs.

I wanted to shoot whoever had put me in this predicament. I had a vision of a tattooed freak with long stringy black hair and a goatee. The image didn't sit well with me. It stirred the anger up even more. Somehow, the faceless, nameless vision had known I was taking the boat out, and I certainly wasn't happy with the end result.

My anger gave me a newfound burst of energy, so I lifted the object one more time—I was almost exhausted now, my lungs had started to fill with water, my mind drew blanks, and the darkness had started coming for me. I coughed—I knew I was getting close to the end. Despite the darkness I saw a bright light, didn't know up from down, and I saw a single moment of my life flash before my eyes. I jammed my lifeline against the shackle one more time, coughing as I did so, knowing that *this was it for me*, that I would die without seeing Lana naked, despite her best efforts to show me what she was made of, without ever knowing the real story about Jessica Mason's death, without knowing the true nature surrounding Cindy Bell's demise, without knowing which dancers were telling the truth and which dancers weren't—if any of them were—with salt water stinging my eyes, with the number of naked women I'd slept with at less than triple digits, letting a case get away from me, letting a stupid case be the end of me. I kicked, wiggled, and squirmed, figuring if I was going down, I was going to shimmy my way into heaven, or at least dance my way out of hell.

And that's when the chain broke.

I kicked and pumped my way to the surface, following the bubbles from my last cough as I went. By the time I breathed fresh air, I thought I still might choke and die. I'd almost choked to death on a piece of steak when I was eight, and I thought I was going to pass out and die then—I didn't—and I wasn't going to die now either. I was determined to live. That single factor saved me from multiple brushes with death, some more intense than others, all of them quite a ride, all of them bound and determined to suck the last breath out of my lungs, and all of them had failed.

When I was able to breathe somewhat normally again, I looked around. I was all alone. The boat was gone, Lana was gone, and the shore was nowhere in sight—but it was still dark, so I couldn't be sure. The lump on my head had started to swell. Confusion engulfed my thoughts with disorientation coming in a close second. My vision blurred, and I thought I might pass out all over again, sinking below the surface once more. *How did I get in this predicament?* With my head bobbing just above the surface, the knot on my head hurting like a mother, and waves cresting all around me, I spun in a circle to reorient myself and capture what was left of my bearings.

Based on the bump on my head, the object that hit me must have been solid, not just a fist but something with more force behind it. It wouldn't have surprised me if my attacker had decided to hit me over the head with my own gun—the dirty prick—and then he either kept it or tossed it in the water along with me. Of course, if a blunt object had been my downfall, I couldn't rule out a *she* either. After all, there were more than enough people that wanted me dead, and not all of them were male.

And I couldn't decide if I'd been betrayed by Lana Ralstein, a great actress putting on a great show, or if Lana might have had to swim her way to freedom—or worse. I didn't like the thought of my witness being taken away from me.

Another wave crested around me, and my vision cleared just enough for me to see the dim lights of the shoreline. I treaded water for a few more minutes until I got tangled in a wave big enough to take me to shore. My arms, legs, and lungs protested the entire trip.

I had no idea who wanted me dead, but I did know I would get even. And I wouldn't stop until I did.

29

"You look like hell!" Ian Jackard said.

"I had t–to swim," I said, still coughing. I resisted the urge to shake myself dry like a dog, although it might have been fun to see Ian get sprayed.

He could have tried to toss me back in the water—he wouldn't have had much luck.

"From where?"

"I d–don't, don't want to talk about it—now," I said.

"Do you need some sleep?" Ian had shown up less than ten minutes ago, and he'd already given me more crap than I deserved. First, he wasn't happy about being called after ten—I'd found a pay phone near the boardwalk; my cell phone and car keys were at the bottom of the ocean floor, along with my pride, waiting on a miracle. Second, he didn't appreciate the fact that I'd called him collect, although that was a more restricted protest. Then he told me I shouldn't have been out on the water in the first place, that the weather wasn't ideal for boating. He wondered why I even bothered courting one of the dancers, saying I was too close to the crime. Finally, he told me wet didn't mesh well with his leather seats, that he'd just had his car detailed.

"I need a lot of things," I said. I couldn't pinpoint every last one of them. Answers, however, were near the top of the list—and I had even more waiting in the wings.

I couldn't figure out what had happened; my head wrung like a steel drum; I sneezed ocean water; my lips were salt-filled and dry; even my shoes were soaked; numbness had set in; and my memory was shot.

I couldn't remember the time between being knocked on the head and coming to in the water, clawing my way back to the surface. What I wanted to know was why I had taken a swan dive off my own rented boat, and what, if anything, Lana Ralstein had to do with it. Either I would get myself killed or I'd discover the truth, and I had no idea which would come first. Otherwise, I needed a long, hot shower.

"Your eyes are bloodshot."

"I'm glad you noticed," I said. We hadn't moved from our spot on the pier. If he wanted to wait for me to dry, I'd toss him in the water, and then I'd commandeer his vehicle. It wasn't my Viper, but it would have to do.

"And you couldn't possibly be more drenched if you stood out in a hurricane."

I said, "You don't miss a thing." I hacked up more sea water.

"There's no need for attitude," Ian said. "I can leave your butt on this pier, and you can find your own way home. If you'd have looked harder, I'm sure you could find your boat. You probably didn't even try."

"It was borrowed." Like the way I was living my life—on borrowed time.

"It's gone." Ian stared out at the water. He probably wanted the boat to appear out of the mist, come toward the shore, and me to hop on it.

"Like I said, you don't miss a thing."

"I try not to," he said. "It must be the lieutenant in me."

"You're not a lieutenant," I said. "You're a detective. There's a big difference. You might want to take a few more notes. Plus, you shouldn't misrepresent yourself, it's bad for publicity."

"There's no need to get nasty."

Ian squinted, and then Ian stared. Neither of which was particularly attractive or endearing.

I, however, felt like my head was coming out of my ears.

"I can handle a lot of things," Ian said. "So far, I've been able to handle you. But if you're feeling lonely, I'm sure we could move your services elsewhere. There's a big ocean out there, and apparently your name is written all over it."

"Maybe you're the one who's lonely." I decided not to point out that I was a wounded man who had a jackrabbit heart rate, arms that clung to my sides, and hair that had probably lost most of its gel.

"I don't get lonely," he said. "I have a wife."

"My point exactly." That was all the reason I'd need to feel extremely lonely.

Ian just shook his head. He was out of witty comebacks. My breath was getting short and coming in gasps. I'd probably overexerted myself on the swim back to shore; I hoped it wasn't delayed drowning from all the salt water I'd inhaled.

It was a long swim, and I told myself I needed the exercise. I hadn't gone swimming in months, my arms stroking through the ocean, the waves slapping at my butt, and now I could say I had. I decided to let Ian do the honor of driving me home, even though Morgan Freeman drove faster when he drove Miss Daisy.

I licked my finger and held it out to the side. "Yep, it's going to be a rough night tonight. You might want to kick the speedometer above thirty. Otherwise, all the old ladies will zoom past you like you were standing still."

"Who said I was giving you a ride?" His comment came a little late—he was already driving me home. Ian had the habit of being a bit slow, not just in his driving.

I felt safe, not because of Ian's propensity for the slow lane, but I wasn't sure how long the feeling would last. Safety flitted like a trash bag blowing away in the breeze, and I had a lump on the back of my head from some unknown individual that I needed to rectify, presumably someone taller than myself, since the lump was large. I hadn't even seen it coming.

My panting began to decrease dramatically. I didn't like being winded, and I didn't like being knocked over the head. In either case I hadn't been given a choice. What I did know, though, was that I could still hold my breath for two minutes, and that running helped my lung capacity. I needed to run more and get knocked over the head less.

I watched a slew of cars pass us. An old guy in a green Cadillac was giving us a run for our money. Another red light appeared overhead. I was pretty sure we'd managed to hit every one in a six block radius. It might have been seven. And I probably needed to stop counting.

"So what have you learned?" I asked. I'd already given him the full story, not the half-assed one.

"I was going to ask you the same thing."

"You don't mix business with pleasure," I said. "It's a hazardous sport, and even I have my limits of how far I'm willing to go—"

"I could have told you that one a long time ago. It doesn't matter anyway. You never were very good at listening to reason." It was his attempt at humor. I thought it was humorous that he didn't take his eyes off the road when he talked. That was probably a good thing. He really needed to watch what he was doing when he hit twenty-five miles an hour.

"I listen."

Ian said, "I was thinking—"

"That's a bad sign when you do that. You're going to start killing your brain cells. From what I know you only have about five or six left, and you want to keep every last one of them. If you get lucky, they'll multiply."

"How long can you hold your breath?"

"For about two minutes," I said. "Why?"

"Just curious. No matter what happens you always resurface. I don't think you could be killed with silver bullets and a three-fifty-seven. I bet vampires are easier to kill than you are, and they're less annoying, too. Maybe you were a werewolf in your previous life, and now you've come back to haunt my dreams."

I choked back a laugh, and I coughed more water out of my lungs. A few more coughs and I'd be at full capacity. And then I'd be as dangerous as ever. "You never know. One gets lucky once in a while."

"You seem to get luckier than most. Maybe you should start playing the lottery."

"Why did you accept my call?"

I'd called him collect from a pay phone. I'd lost my wallet in the swim and my gun before that, and I'd lost Lana Ralstein before I lost my wallet or my gun. Along with the wallet and gun, I'd managed to lose my car keys and cell phone. I couldn't think of a single thing I'd won, except a ride home with Ian, and I didn't even like him. But I kept him around because he was a lot of fun. No, wait, I had that backward. I shook my head.

"That's the last time I accept a collect call from you," he said. "If I'd have known you weren't going to dry off in the fresh air, I would have told you to find your own ride. I'm not running some kind of charity."

"So what have you found out for me?" I asked. I did my best not to drip or shiver. I wasn't doing a very good job of either. Without even thinking Ian had turned on the air conditioner. I didn't look in the mirror because I was afraid my lips were blue.

He slammed on the brakes. I guess it didn't bother him that we were on a main stretch of road, cars all around us. One or two horns honked, and one or two fingers were probably popped up in the distinctive gesture of love and affection. It had gained in popularity, and with the avid use of cell phones, it only had the potential to get bigger.

I had deposited my cell phone at the bottom of the ocean, and I smiled at the thought of a sting ray dialing one of my ex-girlfriends.

"You might want to step on the gas," I said. "We're getting strange looks. And I think some old woman gave us the finger. She's been trying to pass us for two minutes."

"Shut up."

"That's all you can come up with?"

"You talk too much," Ian said.

And that's all he said for several minutes. I wasn't sure what had gotten under his skin. It might have been my shivering, or it might have been my dripping. I didn't think it was my talking. Ian was pretty tolerant.

The car lurched forward, and when he wasn't paying attention, I turned on the heat. He didn't notice. Ian didn't notice much at the moment. He stared straight ahead, hands gripping the steering wheel as tightly as possible, an odd smirk on his face, his eyes wild. He had a look of pure determination, anger, excitement, and fear, all rolled into one little package of pure driving bliss.

"So what have the two nitwits found out?" A common reference for Mayberry and Stephens.

"Probably not as much you," Ian said. "Otherwise you wouldn't have taken a swim in the ocean and currently be dripping all over my leather upholstery."

"Then I'm still not sure who pulled the trigger. My last conversation, before I took a dip, was with Lana Ralstein, and before that it was Derrick Stevens. While Derrick has a temper that rivals most rabid squirrels, I'm not sure he's the murderer. And Lana doesn't fit the profile. She had no motive to whack Jessica Mason that I've been able to find. And I've hit a snag in the dancer suicide that took place fourteen years ago."

"What suicide?" Ian said. He jerked the car over to the side of the road, almost cutting off a minivan and a BMW, and then he shut off the engine.

I told him about Cindy.

When I was finished, his face turned three shades paler.

"What do you know about it?" I said.

"That case was filed away with authority," he said. "When I have a spare moment, I'll take a peek at it, and maybe I'll find what everyone else has missed, since it never really sat right with me. And I could never pinpoint exactly why. Just a hunch, more than anything else."

"That's the same feeling I had. And the only link between the two seems to be Veronica Sutton. None of the dancers were with the VDC fourteen years ago. Heck, none of them had hit high school. Veronica knew about Jessica Mason's pregnancy, the only one I've been able to find so far, except for possibly the father, Bradley Cassidy, and I haven't spoken to him yet.

"While Bradley, Kathryn, and Derrick are still suspects in Jessica's death, as far as I can tell none of them killed Cindy, nor did they have a reason to." That I'd been able to find. "If Cindy's death wasn't a suicide, then there's a good chance it might have been Veronica. Cindy Bell wanted to get pregnant; she didn't use drugs; even her boyfriend was clean; she mentioned leaving the VDC to Veronica; she also dropped that she wanted to get pregnant; and not long after that, she ended up dead.

"What still bugs me, though, is Bradley. Someone stuck him in front of the firing squad and is ready to pull the trigger. If I finger him, then Cindy's death doesn't change, and I'm back at the drawing board. But he's the father of Jessica's unborn child; he lost his watch at the crime scene; his saliva might very well be attached to Jessica's vagina; and if he didn't want the kid, that'd be more than enough reason to whack Ms. Mason." And I still had my other problem: Somebody wanted to whack me, too.

"Often the cleanest answer isn't the right one," Ian said.

30

"You're not around much," Alexandra Bridges said.

It was true—I wasn't. I'd gotten wrapped up in my case, and just a little less than a week ago we'd spent more than a month together. I'd been splitting my time between the case, Lana, and Beverly, and I didn't have as much room for Alexandra right now. I couldn't tell her all the reasons, so I said, "I didn't know it was required."

"You're missing out on all the fun."

"When you put it like that," I said, "I feel like I'm depriving myself of something good." It was also a moot point to mention that I was making the time for her now. Women didn't understand the in-between time, even if they were independent.

Ian had dropped me off, and since I didn't want to spend the night alone, I called Alexandra. She had arrived at my doorstep before we hung up, so I took that as a good sign. Little did I know I had the game all wrong, and I needed to play catch-up before she yelled checkmate and stole all of my pieces.

"You are missing something good," she said.

"Glad to see you don't think too highly of yourself," I said. I also happened to think very highly of myself. I didn't want to sell myself short of a good time, nor did I want the past to catch up with me. The past was a wild ride that I lived through once, and I wasn't sure

I could make it through a second round. I only had enough pieces to solve one or two puzzles, not three or four.

Her smile appeared, and it would have knocked me down if I didn't have wicked thoughts of Lana on my mind. Despite the unusual circumstance of our departure, she wasn't an easy thought to get rid of.

"I try not to," Alexandra said.

"You might want to try a little harder next time."

"Didn't you learn that the relationship is all about the woman? Or are you still letting your stubbornness get the better of you?"

"I must have missed that section of the book. I probably used it for firewood. Could you repeat some of the key points?"

"You're a firecracker."

I took a step toward her. We'd been standing on opposite sides of my living room, and she'd been giving me funny looks the whole time, except for the smile that appeared and disappeared. Her dark hair was smooth and silky, her eyes were dark points in a midnight sky, and she was only a little over half-dressed.

My big screen TV gave off less energy than her, and my black leather couch appeared ripe for the taking. Of course, if we never made it as far as the sofa, there was always the Berber carpet to consider.

"That's a new one," I said. "I thought only little kids were bundles of energy."

She took a step back. "Last time I checked you could be pretty energetic."

"When I'm not knee deep in a case," I said. I always knew what she had in mind when it came to bedroom activities. She didn't do subtlety very well—she could scream for all she was worth during sex, and she snored louder than a plane taking off. But as far as her mind, it was locked tighter than a Federal Reserve building.

"Exactly."

"But that doesn't happen very often," I said. I made sure I got my share of vacations, along with a few extra just for good measure. I liked to reward myself. And when I had free time, I liked to reward myself even more.

"Precisely."

"It sounds like someone is jealous. You aren't feeling neglected, are you?"

"I have a right to be," Alexandra said.

I didn't wrap my arms around her—I wasn't the comforting type. "I didn't know you were the jealous type."

"We all have our breaking points," she said.

We'd made it to the couch, and she did her best to keep her distance. I did nothing to alleviate her concerns. She was still a knockout, despite my best efforts to ignore the point. I had on one of my favorite t-shirts, and she didn't even seem to notice. I, on the other hand, noticed her chest as well as all of her other moving parts. They were exposed beneath a knit top and knit bottom. I had the best seat in the house, and there was no way I would ever give it up.

"And it appears I'm finding your breaking point," I said. "I didn't think you had one."

"It's the little things that get you in the end, the details you skip over. You're good at failing to acknowledge the important points."

"I acknowledge a lot of things," I said. I didn't mean to get defensive—I couldn't help myself. I probably still had water in my brain, and I still had rampant sexual thoughts running through every inch of my body. The knit outfit did nothing to alleviate my sexual energy.

"But not the things you need most," she said. The sad look in her eyes said it all—I was pretty sure she'd reached the end of the line. And I'd probably never figure out why. Women never wanted to say why. I'd faced the crushing blow of one or two breakups, and I hadn't received one valid explanation. It was the price I paid for getting involved with women. I consoled myself with the fact that I could always find another. And I kept my giant net handy.

Alexandra hugged herself, and she looked away from me. Off into the distance somewhere, past my sparkling hazel eyes and loud t-shirt. "Why do you always make things difficult?" she asked.

"I didn't know I was."

"Don't tell me you're completely clueless. I don't believe it." She turned away from me. There was something in her eyes—it wasn't happiness. "You're a difficult one. I thought you'd get easier with time, but you're not. I think you're getting harder. You haven't grown up. I don't think you ever will."

I didn't want to point out that I looked young enough to get carded in certain situations, and I'd been mistaken for a college student twice in the past year. "You're going to let the good times go? I thought you enjoyed having a good time. What made you change your mind?"

She shook her head. "Your mind is lost on a giant wave, and I don't think you'll ever get it back. Even when this case is over, you won't be. You'll chase after the next pretty lady that knocks on your door, and one of these days you're going to get yourself killed. I don't want to be around when that happens."

I'd told her about my most recent near death experience, and it chilled her to the bone, even more than it chilled me.

She leaned forward, inches away from me. "I can't wait around on you any longer. I'm not getting any younger, and I haven't managed to sweep the stress out of my life. Instead of making my life easier, you make it more difficult, and despite my hope that it would, my life hasn't improved with you in it."

She didn't have to tell me that I was the stress.

And then she hopped off my couch so fast I thought the momentum might knock her to the ground. It didn't. She walked out the door, and I didn't try to stop her. I told myself I didn't need her; I told myself I didn't want her; I told myself I could do without her. All comforting thoughts, and I had a feeling they were all lies. I could no longer separate the lies from the truth when it came to women, and what little truth I did have, I watched disappear in a cloud of smoke.

When I lost Kayla Indigo, my high school sweetheart, I lost a part of myself I could never get back. Kayla was all I had, and now I had nothing. I bounced from one relationship to the next hoping to find what I'd lost. I'd been trying to repair the damage for so long I'd forgotten how. I simply covered it up with relationships and women and more relationships and more women. I found myself headed on a one-way track straight out of town, and there was no way to turn my Viper back around.

I wasn't around to hold Kayla. She was killed in a tragic car accident on her way to see me. It was a Friday evening, late, after one of our biggest football games of the year. A driver with a big pickup truck changed lanes without signaling, striking her car on the driver's side and spinning her car out of control. She crossed the median into oncoming traffic, and another car swallowed her whole. She was killed instantly, along with the driver in the other car, and for months I couldn't revive myself. Prom was less than two months away. She died, and then my parents died, and then my life started to get really interesting. But not always in a good way.

When I informed Ian of my missing gun, he told me I needed to have my head examined.

Since I'd been whacked over the head and left for dead, I didn't find his advice particularly amusing. I knew I'd have to file a report, and since I didn't know whether the gun had been stolen or tossed in the drink along with me, the thought wasn't encouraging. But I'd learned to grin and bear it, or so said one of my t-shirts.

Paperwork aside, I probably did need to have my head examined, based on the throbbing that erupted from the less handsome side of my melon. It hurt worse than the time I'd been slapped by three women at once—a story best saved for another time—and I now had a knot on the back of my head the size of a giant cockroach. My head swam with possibilities about my dive over the side, and unfortunately, not very many answers. And the ringing in my ears didn't make the answers flow any easier.

Since I knew only one female doctor intimately (it wasn't from a lack of trying with the others), I decided to call Isabel Titler in my hour of need. Before I could avail myself of her services, it took a bit of convincing on my part, but I didn't have to resort to begging.

While I waited for her arrival, I applied a bag of frozen mixed vegetables to the back of my head; it didn't affect the bump, but it did manage to turn my head ten shades colder. Less than a defrosted package later, Isabel greeted me in a white lab coat that ended just below her knees, her blond hair pulled back from her face, her red lips puckered (that might have been my imagination), and a grin that was just this side of sly.

She rushed inside before I could extend forth the invitation. She stood opposite me in my living room, her arms draped at her sides. Just before she placed them on her slim hips, she appraised my situation. "What have you managed to do to yourself now?"

"I can assure you, schweetheart, it wasn't me." I attempted a Humphrey Bogart accent, which didn't work.

"Don't call me sweetheart again, or I might be forced to rip out your tongue." Her evil eye told me she was serious.

I shrugged my shoulders. "It's a figure of speech."

She shook her head, tossed her coat on the arm of my sofa—then ripped off her blouse (the last part was only in my mind, but it was a wonderful image). "You're more trouble than you even realize."

I happened to know just how much trouble I was, since I'd been apprised of my worth on multiple occasions, and one 2005 Dodge Viper SRT-10 seemed like a small price to pay for a lifetime of adventure.

As to the current whereabouts of my Viper, I was strictly in denial and would have resorted to a period of mourning if not for the throbbing in my head. It sent cold rivulets from my head to the tips of my toes as I considered what might happen to the fire-engine red goddess before I could safely return it to my possession. As for the boat, the worst I would lose was the deposit—and possibly an eardrum from the bean-counting insurance adjuster who would assault my humble ears with endless questions. Paying extra for the insurance package, along with handing over a wad of cash to grease the wheels, had proved to be pure genius, even if it meant my yachting days might have come to an abrupt end. The sound of an engine taking hold and the thought of bikinis drifting toward the deck made another part of me ache more than my head.

I still had one baby, though, who presented slapping as a first line of justice, even if she did hold back on this particular occasion. Knowing her and her temper, I pictured a lighted fuse and a barrel filled with dynamite. She had a slightly empathetic expression painted on her face, but it could have been an act. She quizzed me about various points in my life, presumably for concussion purposes, and I indulged her request without much protest other than a grunt or two. Satisfied, she abandoned her post for medical supplies, leaving me to my own devices and thoughts of a missing yacht.

That *Big Bertha* drifted off into the sunset without yours truly on board nagged at me, but not as much as the pounding in my brain and the lack of outer attire on my blond partner (she had stripped off her sweatshirt), who had shoved me onto the couch and dug her nails into my shoulders hard enough to force me to lie back. When she brought out the needle, I turned my head away. At least she had given me a shot of Jose Cuervo Gold before she plunged the needle home with what I believed was more than a little too much enthusiasm on her part. If my head had been pointed in her direction, I might have caught a wicked gleam in her eye.

I rubbed my right arm, since she still had her fingernails entrenched in my left one, the contents of the needle fading from existence. "Do you even know what you're doing?"

"I've beaten you at Operation seven times in a row, haven't I?" The contests were rigged; she had delicate piano fingers, while mine were a bit wider than hers.

"What's the shot for again?"

"I know how much you love needles." She rubbed the back of my head with some combination of iodine and rubbing alcohol that nearly knocked me back out, the odor worse than a swift kick to the groin from a woman named Sandy.

"You had a concussion," Isabel said, "and the lump on the back of your head is about the size of a walnut. Otherwise, you're going to be fine."

"Can I trust you?" I asked. I still had the distinct impression she took great pleasure in what had happened to me. The bag of mixed vegetables might have also offered support.

"Why did you call me in the first place?" She asked as she examined my eyes again, staring hard into the pupils, her right hand pinching my cheek.

"Because I was running out of options," I said, "and I knew I could count on you."

She slapped me on the cheek, hard, and the ringing in my ears returned with a vengeance.

"You're still the same bastard you always were."

"Yes," I said, "but now I'm a smarter bastard and a more efficient one as well."

But smart though I may have been, I still wasn't any closer to my assailant or the murderer, assuming the two were somehow connected. That might have been a big assumption, or it might not have been. Either way, I wanted to march arm-in-arm with the truth, right up the middle aisle. Being alive, though, sounded a whole lot more appealing than being dead.

She shoved a couple of capsules in my mouth—not the little blue pills—and handed me a glass of water from the tap. "So where's your girlfriend?"

I swallowed the pills and water and handed the glass back to her.

"What are you talking about?"

"Don't play dumb with me," she said. "I know you had a woman on the boat with you."

"Are you psychic?"

"No, but I know you a little too well. Probably better than I should, actually."

She did know me, better than I did. But it wasn't from a lack of trying on my part. She had been reluctant to give up the goods like most of my prime witnesses, all of whom told some doctored version of the truth in an effort to serve their own needs and disrupt mine.

I told Isabel I had no idea where the woman was—or if she was even alive—and that I didn't remember much about events immediately before I was clocked over the head. My memory gap was several minutes long, and as far as I knew, the boat was several miles offshore. Not that we had started out that way. Lana did her best to flag down the Coast Guard with her yellow bikini top.

My biggest issue, however, was that someone wanted me dead, and I had no idea how I would dance my way out of that one.

She said, "That's par for the course, isn't it?"

"You don't even golf," I said. And I didn't either. I lacked the patience to chase a little white ball all over the course, through sand traps and high grass and moats that guarded the prized greens.

"Neither do you."

It was true. I decided we had already talked about golf much longer than I would have liked and changed tactics. "What would you do if I died?"

She pressed a finger to her lips before she spoke. "I could give your eulogy."

I smiled. "You'd do that for me?"

"I might consider it."

"Maybe you should stay over—"

She stood up rather abruptly. "I don't think so."

"In case I need a doctor in the middle of the night or the person who wants to kill me decides to come back. Besides, with a concussion, don't I need to be evaluated every hour?" I tried a pitiful expression, but it appeared I was unsuccessful with that as well.

"You've gotta be kidding me," she said. "If *you're* helpless, then I'm Pope John Paul II."

I decided to point out the obvious. "He's dead."

"And you're lucky you're not. But luck has helped you out of more than a jam or two."

I tried another tactic. "What about giving me a thorough examination?"

"You can't be serious."

"I'm always serious," I said. "After all, it's what I do best."

"I'm leaving," Isabel said. "If you have any other injuries in the course of this investigation, don't bother calling me."

I smiled and gave my helpless-guy face one more shot.

She didn't buy it.

31

I slept alone, and I wasn't happy about it. My head felt as though I'd downed twenty-one shots of tequila on my twenty-first birthday: I wasn't pleased with the end result and neither was my head. I started off my day with sit-ups, push-ups, a four mile run, a cold shower, two cups of coffee, a change of clothes, and a new t-shirt. It was the best I could hope for on short notice. The activities forced me to focus, even though my head was still on the island waiting for my boat to return to port. The cold shower helped, just not enough.

As for the port, I did return to the dock, the boards shaking under my feet like a heroin addict; I asked a few questions—most of which were intelligent—after I observed that my missing boat had found its way home; I received several shrugs and a few halfhearted replies; I inspected the vessel myself in all of its bottle cap glory with nary a scratch to be found.

I retrieved my red goddess from the parking lot, minus one taxicab fare, and revved the engine. At least I had my Viper back in my possession. As for the rest of it, I figured it would work itself out, despite the lingering questions in my mind.

Since I'd gone for my swim soon after I left the VDC, and since the VDC had most of the verbal action, I decided to return there, hoping for a little more, minus the swimming part. The getting knocked over the head part wasn't much fun either.

"I thought I'd lost you," she said. She stared at me, her head turned slightly to the side.

"What's going on?" I said. I couldn't have painted the shock any brighter on my face with suntan oil. Or maybe that was my head working out a few kinks. I wanted answers since I couldn't find any in my personal life. The more I tried to figure out what was going on, the more likely it was that I'd end up at the bottom of the ocean, in jail, or minus a girlfriend. I wondered if the truth could really set me free or if it would give me a migraine.

"I'm not even sure I know the whole story."

"Why don't you start with the truth?" I asked. I never got the whole truth from ex-girlfriends, and I was pretty sure I wouldn't get it here. Women had a way of making things more difficult than they really were.

She stood close enough to touch me, and the empty dance room didn't make me want to do the waltz, even though soft rock music came through the speakers. Her eyes had dark spots under them, her face was a shade paler than normal, and her clothes were disheveled. A bandage covered a spot on her forehead.

"I'm not sure I can tell you the truth," Lana Ralstein said. "It might cost me too much."

"Yet you don't mind lying to me. You're great at deceiving me, Lana. You must get all the guys that way. I start out dancing with you, and I end up knocked over the head and tossed over the side. Even my craziest ex-girlfriends didn't try to have me killed, and they had more reasons than you to harm me."

She just shook her head. "You have no idea what you've gotten involved in."

"That's what I'm trying to figure out," I said. "There were two dead dancers, one was ruled a suicide and the other ruled a homicide, and I've got nothing but a sea of suspicious characters." I waited for my head to catch up. "Even the cops won't talk to me, and I happen to know one or two who are still on the force. I've got bits and pieces to a story that still needs a villain. And I visited this studio not long before I took a nosedive off my previously rented yacht." I held off her onslaught with my hand in the air. "An even bigger mystery is the boat showing back up at the dock, unscathed, and no one seems to be the wiser.

"You have a performance in a couple of weeks, and it'll be hard to perform with no dancers left. You might want to start looking for some backup dancers."

My head felt like the needle had been pointed all the way to overdrive, and the ringing in my ears wasn't related to any uppercut I had ever taken on the chin. I placed my hand against the wall before I passed out standing up.

Her face turned bright pink. "I don't know what to tell you. You should have never taken this case in the first place, and you should probably walk away now, but I know you won't. Kathryn Gable had no right to ask for your help."

"It's not that I won't," I said. "It's that I can't." I crossed my arms. "And there's nothing wrong with being concerned about your lover." I changed tactics and willed my brain to keep up. "By the way, what happened to your head?"

She just shook her head, the question lingering in the air like a bout of tuberculosis. "It's not all that hard, really. You should try it some time. All you have to do is say that the case isn't worth all the trouble it's causing you."

"I've always been bigger than my cases, and I'm not going to change my attitude now. There's too much at stake for me to just jump ship. I could have drowned."

"You're still alive," she said. It didn't sound like there was a hint of remorse in her voice. If that was a bit of a consolation, it wasn't much.

"Yeah, and I'm trying to figure out why you didn't get tossed over the side. For the life of me I can't come up with anything. Even though you're pretty, I don't think you're pretty enough to talk your way out of a drop to the bottom of the ocean."

"How do you know I wasn't?" she said.

Lana had a point. I couldn't remember anything between being knocked over the head and waking up at the bottom. It didn't take the detective in me to figure out I'd been dropped like a banana peel. Although when it came to women, I normally got the drop on them, not the other way around.

"So what do you think?" she asked.

"I don't know."

Lana said, "Well, let me know when you figure it out."

I nodded, and she walked away.

I hoped to get smarter by osmosis. It didn't work. I wandered around the studio, with the long corridor almost like a second home to me, and I bumped into Bradley Cassidy. Since he needed to give me a few answers, I figured luck was on my side.

He had on a headband, tights, and ribbed polyester t-shirt; I had on jeans, loafers, and one of my famous t-shirts.

He smirked. "You haven't given up, have you?"

"Not on your life," I said. "This is more fun than going to the movies. All I need now is the big bang at the end of the film."

"You're one sick individual," he said.

I nodded. "Maybe I am. I was always told I didn't play well with others."

"Do you know the meaning of the word quit?"

"No, I've heard the word before, but it's not really part of my vocabulary. Plus, I happen to enjoy the art of extreme death. It's a bigger rush than bungee jumping." I paused. "You and I have some unfinished business."

"What do you want to know?"

"I heard you fathered a child."

"What? You can't be serious. Where do you get your information?"

His words told me one side of the story, and his reactions told me another. I always focused on the reactions. Words were easy to fake; reactions were much harder.

"Why don't you play it straight with me?" I asked.

"Well, if you already know all the answers, why are you coming to me? Why not just type up your little report and be done with it."

"I was never one for reports. Too much paperwork. And I want all the facts. I don't like walking around half-cocked. I'd rather be fully loaded. Thorough is my middle name. I want to know more than who, I want to know why."

"I've already seen you in a t-shirt that said something to that effect."

"I have a lot of t-shirts," I said. "I'm just trying to keep my options open."

He placed his right hand against the wall. "You're worse than a bloodsucking leech. I'd have an easier time facing a Mack truck head on."

"I wouldn't recommend it. Too messy. Why don't you tell me what's really going on here? Maybe we can save ourselves a bit of trouble."

Bradley said, "Oh, is that all you're after?"

"I want the facts," I said. "All of them."

"The fact is I'm one of three people in love with Jessica." He meant Mason, and he used the present tense. "She was the sun to my stars. I would have given her anything she wanted, and she wanted me to be the father of her child. She told me I had good genes. I'm athletic, flexible, smart, and talented."

"What about your misplaced watch?"

"What about it?" he asked.

"One was found on the body."

"You don't think I killed her—"

"I don't know what to think," I said. "Nothing in life is ever black and white. I live in a gray world, and the longer I'm involved in a case, the grayer it gets. I might as well live in New England and watch the rain every day from my window."

He ignored my comment. Maybe he wasn't a Red Sox fan. "If I were the father of her child, why would I want to get rid of her?"

"Indeed. That's the million dollar question. You're rolling the dice, and I'm dragging the magnet under the table to see which way those three dimensional squares will land. I have a lot of money riding on six."

He folded his arms across his narrow chest; I ran a hand through my hair. He tapped the wall; I tapped my pocket. Both of us looked around; neither of us found anything remotely interesting. I still wanted to know how far dancers could bend over, and I wouldn't have objected to another boob flash.

"Did you get your hair colored?" I asked.

"I had some highlights put in two days ago. You noticed that?"

"I notice everything," I said. Then my hand darted out and yanked one of the hairs out of his head. I stuffed it in my pocket before he even made a sound.

Bradley tapped his head where the hair had been, stuck his chin out, gave me the evil eye, and did an about face.

32

I talked to a dancer or two, peered in on a lesson, waited for breasts to start bouncing, and then I tracked Kathryn Gable back to her office.

"Did you solve the fourteen-year-old murder?" she asked.

"I'm working on it," I said.

She held her arms up high, bent over at the waist and then leaned back. She repeated the process twice, each position was held for ten seconds before she moved on. "How hard?"

"I conducted some research on the Internet," I said, "and I discovered her death was ruled a suicide: The cops never really pursued any other options. Her boyfriend was a user, drugs were found in her system as well as next to her, the boyfriend was a suspect, but the cops ruled foul play wasn't involved. I had conversations with Ty and Evelyn Bell and Gloria Headwitz. Gloria tried to take my clothes off."

"Gloria tries to take everyone's clothes off. Did you see her mirrors?"

"I saw her mirrors, and I saw her purple underwear. I was intrigued, but she's already oversexed the way it is, so I didn't want to throw myself into the mix. I might not have enough sex to go around."

"Do you do any actual detective work?" she asked. "Or do you just picture women naked all day long?"

"I do some detective work," I said. "But it's mostly picturing women naked."

Kathryn was finished with her stretching, so she stepped out of the changing room, and I followed. She found an empty rehearsal room, flicked on the lights, and started having her way with a bar near the front of the room. A light, upbeat song improved my mood, ever so slightly, while I stood guard at the door: I didn't want anyone to think me a student. It would throw my testosterone level out of whack.

"Why do you think the cops didn't get anywhere fourteen years ago?"

"Because they weren't looking in the right places," I said. "People see the world through their own sunglasses, and it's very hard to change their perspective."

"What makes you better than everyone else?"

"I manage to take my sunglasses off once in a while."

Kathryn said, "You don't mind getting blinded by the sun?"

"Not if it helps me find the truth."

She bobbed up and down, and then she did a series of complicated stretches for which arms and legs were splayed in every direction. I watched, fascinated and intrigued. All I could think about was how much my balls would hurt if I tried to mimic her.

"And that's all you're after?" she asked.

"Well, I'd like to make the world a better place—"

"By screwing everything with a heartbeat?"

I bit my lip and stared.

"Casey, don't assume you're the only one who does his homework. Before I get involved with anyone, I figure out who they really are."

I found her choice of words interesting. "You're not going to try and beat me at my own game, are you?"

"I wouldn't dream of it," she said. She popped up like a twenty dollar bill. "Do you think it was a suicide?" She meant Cindy's untimely demise.

"I'm beginning to believe there was a good chance it wasn't."

"Well," she said, "that's a much better conclusion than the cops ever reached. Maybe they should have held up little white flags."

"You can't compare me to everyone else. I'm about as far from normal as you can get and still be considered sane." All I needed was the t-shirt to prove it.

"I'm beginning to see the truth in that statement."

She'd glided across the floor toward me, and she now stood just outside of my personal space barrier, which retracts inward when women are involved. She tapped her thigh; I waited her out. She gave up before I did.

"You must have sought me out for a reason . . ."

"Is there anyone currently at the studio who was here fourteen years ago?"

"Why?" she asked.

"I'd like to unravel more thread, and I think I'm down to the last few strands. If I don't figure this all out soon, I'll have to start pulling out the reserves."

"Only one person that I'm aware of," she said. "Ollie Nuber."

"Great," I said. "My day just keeps getting better and better. You should have mentioned a woman."

"Casey, do you have a thing for Ollie?"

"No, but I think he has a thing for me," I said. "And it's a pretty big thing, I'm afraid. I'll need a flak vest to talk to him."

Kathryn laughed. It was rather pleasant, constricted, and it ended after two short bursts like a double tap. "You don't seem like the type to exhibit fear."

"I'm not," I said.

Since my case didn't have any choice, and since I put the case first, I decided to set the creep factor aside. Ollie told me he had an office in the studio. It was at the end of a short corridor, away from the rest of civilization, in an area that was less traveled by, and it was an area I had avoided until now.

His office had mine beat on the minimalist factor. It was the size of a large closet and about as pleasant. I stood guard at the door in case I needed to bolt. If Ollie got up from his desk, I wanted a running head start.

"Have you come to take me up on my proposition?" he asked.

"And what proposition would that be?"

"My dinner one."

"I don't eat," I said. And for all he knew, I didn't drink either.

"You don't eat, and you don't drink. You must lead a very dull life." He had a diagram in front of him, and he drew little circles on it. There was a stack of papers near it. I assumed it was the dance routine.

"You have no idea how dull my life is."

His head popped up. "Now I know you're lying."

"Everyone has to play the hand they are dealt. I'm playing against a full house, so my odds aren't real good. I'm hoping for a straight flush or four of a kind."

"And what hand do you want to deal me?"

I ignored the question. "I want to ask you some questions about fourteen years ago. I need to know about Cindy Bell's apparent suicide."

Ollie said, "I wondered when you might get around to asking."

"So it sounds like I've got the right person."

He nodded. "I'm the only one who's still around. Veronica goes through personnel like a drill sergeant at boot camp. If you don't make the grade, you're out on the street before you can even pack up your office. She might ship your personal items to you—or she might not.

"Cindy was one of the best dancers I'd ever seen in my life. She had the body, the talent, and she could bend her body into any position imaginable."

A few ideas popped in my head, a few positions I wouldn't mind trying.

"She could have danced in Europe or Russia, New York or L.A., but she wanted to stay here. She grew up here, and her family was more important to her than prestige and a bigger paycheck.

"She didn't kill herself. I refuse to believe it. She wouldn't touch caffeine or nicotine, so why would she put cocaine in her body? Where would it get her?"

"Dead," I said. "If you don't know what you're doing."

"Cindy knew exactly what she was doing. Always did."

"So what else can you tell me about Veronica Sutton?"

His hand shook for just a second. "She does what she needs to do. If you cross her, you might as well start picking out your own casket."

So why might they cross her? "Then why do you stick with her?" I asked. "You seem talented enough."

"Because she gives me a lot of freedom, the pay is good, and I have no problem respecting authority. And I like the area. New York is overcrowded and full of snow, and L.A. is overcrowded and full of smog."

"That's where you and I differ," I said. "Authority is highly overrated."

"Your arms are well-toned," Ollie said.

"That's so I can strangle people easily."

He laughed. It sounded like a large man choking on a doughnut.

"I bet you say that to all the women," he said.

"It's how I get them," I said. "I charm their panties right off."

"One day your charm will fade, your hair will go gray, you'll get a little soft around the middle, and the panties will stay on."

I gasped. "I plan to stay young and thin forever. And one day I'll have a trophy case full of women's undergarments."

Ollie shook his head. "You should learn to expand your horizons."

"My horizon has expanded as far as it needs to go," I said. "So how did Veronica act after Cindy's death?"

"I don't know. She didn't show up back at the studio for about a week. Never did find out what happened. I suppose she took some sort of extended vacation."

"And when she returned?" I asked.

"She acted as though nothing had ever happened. After all, we were in the middle of rehearsing for a performance, and as they say, the show must go on. In her absence, her assistant took over, and of course, when Veronica returned, she vetoed every decision her assistant made."

"She doesn't seem like the type of person to just up and leave on a whim. What about her assistant? Is she still around?"

"Last I heard she was in California," Ollie said.

"Would you consider Veronica capable of committing murder?"

"She could strangle a python with her bare hands."

Since I was in the mood for python, I sought out Veronica Sutton. Her office was neat, organized, and it had a sterile feel, similar to an empty hospital room. I had an urge to toss a couple papers on the floor to throw the room back in balance.

"You should come with a warning label," she said.

"I could, but the label might not do me justice."

"Does your sense of justice have to collide with my performance schedule?"

"I hoped it wouldn't," I said, "but I can't control my case any more than you can control your dancers."

"I control my dancers just fine. You need to learn to relax a little bit. I have ways that don't even have names, and I bet I'm more experienced than your typical conquest."

"I'm sure you are," I said. "And I have no doubt you're as flexible as you were twenty years ago." I shivered slightly at the thought.

"Well, I'm not quite that flexible," she said. "But I have not forgotten how to have a good time." Her fingers flew over the keys, as I tried not to consider what other uses her fingers might possess. The nails were extra sharp similar to a cougar's teeth.

I said, "Can you really strangle a python?"

"What kind of a question is that?"

"I have no idea," I said. "I'm rather proud of my overactive imagination."

33

I bumped into two dancers on my way out the door. Both of them were female, and neither one of them offered to bend over for me. My charm had failed me, and I needed a new dose of fantasy.

My Viper was right where I left it, the last car in the lot. I clicked open my doors, hopped in the driver's seat, and decided to find out if the hair I'd plucked matched the saliva on Jessica's body—right after I swung by the police station. Ian had left some annoying message on my cell phone, which I deleted immediately.

At the police station I filled out all the appropriate paperwork on my missing firearm, glaring at him the whole time, even when I signed on the dotted line. As to the current whereabouts of said weapon—and unlike the miraculous boat appearance—it was probably still swimming at the bottom of the ocean in a shark's mouth, increasing his metallic content. After I finished the paperwork, and he finished lecturing me on the proper disposal of firearms, I saw myself out.

Since I still remembered where Isabel Titler lived, and after staring at Ian for too many minutes as I perfected my harsh stare, I decided to make an unannounced house call about saliva deposits. She lived in a modern townhouse community with one of those community watch programs.

"You're making house calls now?"

I was feeling as frisky as ever—I tried to hide it. I wasn't sure if it worked or not. If Isabel and I had still been on solid ground, I might have taken it upon myself to act upon my friskiness. As it was, I'd have to do without. I could exercise restraint when I needed to; however, most of the time I didn't.

"It's part of the service we provide," I said. My sparkling white teeth flashed like a Dodge Durango high beam. "We're very thorough, and we do one hell of a job."

"And what service would that be?" Isabel asked. She had greeted me at the door in a white bathrobe tied at the waist, with her hair messed up, and I knew with almost absolute certainty that she wasn't wearing a thing beneath it. I felt a slight stirring below the waist. I started to recite the alphabet backward to keep myself out of trouble.

"Full frontal," I said.

"So says your shirt," she said.

"I picked it out for that specific reason. My wardrobe may appear unplanned to the untrained eye, but I plan my outfits out with extreme precision."

"You probably had other reasons in mind," she said. "All you have to do is throw on a pair of jeans from Abercrombie, American Eagle, or the Gap, and then dig out a t-shirt from your overstocked stash. It's not difficult work."

"Can we stick to the script?" I said. I still had an agenda, and I needed to get through it before I got sidetracked and couldn't pull myself back out. With women it happened more frequently than I liked to admit. Women in white bathrobes only made the situation worse. And beautiful women did it on purpose.

Isabel said, "What script?"

"Can we talk inside?" I tried my low-beam smile. "I need your help."

"As long as you promise not to jump my bones."

"You're so skinny I'd probably break you," I said. She wasn't entirely skinny—I liked my women to have a few curves—and she could still fill out a bathrobe better than several women I'd known. My imagination always got the best of me.

She stepped aside. "Or I could try to break you."

I saluted her as I stepped through the front door.

I thought I looked good. Isabel looked a whole lot better, and I wasn't sure what to do with my assessment. Her messed up hair only seemed to accentuate her high cheekbones, sharp nose, and bronzed skin. I liked bronzed skin, and I liked blond hair. It's a deadly combination, so I made it a habit to stay as far away as possible.

She'd ushered me into the living room. I was on the couch, and she was in her favorite chair with a high back and soft pillow cushions. The living room had pink overtones, a glass coffee table that was more expensive than my outfit, and a flat screen TV that made me jealous. The carpet, however, wasn't quite up to my standards, and even though the pink was subtle, I still felt as though I was in the middle of a birthday cake. Although I'd stand there with my ones at the ready if Isabel decided to pop out of a cake and yank off her bathrobe. In fact, maybe I should've closed the blinds, just in case.

She'd crossed her legs, and I hadn't missed the part where her robe slid up her thigh exposing bare flesh. I tried to calm down my heart, so I looked higher. I'd need a cold shower later—I was glad I hadn't taken one already. And I'd need a hot bout of sex. I was pretty sure that could be arranged as well. I always had a willing participant or two handy for emergencies.

She peered out at me underneath her eyelashes. It was a sexy look, and I recalled her using it recently. I'd been trying to forget stuff like that. I would have liked to have forgotten a lot of things; Isabel Titler was one of those things I couldn't easily forget.

"You know, if you don't close your mouth, you're going to drool all over your t-shirt," Isabel said. "I know you have a whole stack of them, but you might want to keep that one. It looks good on you."

It was a slim fit, and it had just the slightest hint of elastic. It was one of my favorites: They all were. I smiled. I aimed for my devilish grin. Compliments from beautiful women never got old no matter how often I heard them.

"Don't take the compliment to your head. If your head swells any bigger, I'm going to take back every nice thing I've ever said about you. And since you left me high and dry, there aren't as many as there were before."

"That'd be a lot of nice things." I didn't dwell on the "high and dry" comment.

"Not as many as you've said about me."

I smiled again. "You're a tough customer. You always were in another league."

"A woman has to be," she said. "It's a world filled with and run by testosterone. I have to take what I can get. Chivalry has gone out the window, and all good men are taken. The rest of us get the leftover scrubs."

Maybe she meant scraps. I decided not to ask. "Well, then, it's a good thing I've got my fair share. I wouldn't want to start dating the second string."

She chose to ignore my comment. "You have *more* than *most*."

She emphasized more and most. I paused to notice each emphasis. "You always were a charmer, better than I ever gave you credit for. Are you sure I can't tempt you toward a small bit of fun?" She and I both knew what the word fun entailed.

Isabel shook her head. She smoothed out her bathrobe and inched it lower. "You were always as sneaky as that devilish grin of yours," she said. "What did you really come here for?"

"Well, I didn't just come to stare at the merchandise." I whipped out the hair—conveniently protected in a small plastic bag that I had found in the glove compartment of my car.

"What is that?"

"Another DNA sample for you to analyze. I'll bet you your bathrobe this one's a winner. You might as well go ahead and untie it."

"Not so fast, slugger. Did this one get obtained through illegal means as well?"

"Well, Bradley wasn't just going to give it to me. I had to give him a little push. And I needed to give his head a hard yank."

"You know, what scares me the most is that you were a cop once. There are rules, chains of command, and ethics to consider. You might as well go rogue and start working for the CIA. You know, on second thought, I'm not even sure they'd take you. Even the CIA has standards."

"When you need answers, you don't have time to waste on forms and bureaucracy. Have you seen how slowly the court system works? I could kill a guy tomorrow, and it'd be six years before I even stood trial. I could be in Bermuda, living on the beach, soaking up the sun and bikinis, with my surfboard right beside me."

"Now you're just exaggerating," Isabel said.

"Would you rather find out the truth, or would you rather follow the rules?"

"I'd rather follow the rules," she said.

"Now, I know you're lying. I've seen you in action. You gave cops a reason to chase after college women, and they've never stopped lacking reasons since. You once had sex on public property in broad daylight, and you gave a cop—"

She held up her hand. "That was a long time ago." She cinched her robe tighter at the waist. "Do you like what you see?"

"Always."

"Too bad you can't do anything about it."

I leaned forward. "You don't want me to do anything about it." I changed subjects on her, since the look on her face told me I had a better chance of hearing the Pope sing in the Italian opera. "What about my hair?"

"It looks nice," she said. "One day you should think about changing the unkempt look. Spiked hair is going out of style. You were always a little behind the power curve, and you're always a little faster than you appear at first glance."

"No, I meant the hair I gave you."

She winked. And then she stood up. "I'll compare it to the saliva sample." She walked toward her kitchen, leaving me stranded on the sofa, and then she looked back over her shoulder. "I suppose this is a rush job."

"Is there any other kind?" I asked.

When I decided she wasn't coming back, I saw myself out.

34

My Viper still had a few more miles left on it, and since Cindy Bell's parents, Ty and Evelyn, wanted to know where the case took me, I figured they were due for an update. It might have been a bit premature, but I'd rather be early than late, and I'd rather let them know the progress I had made. Cindy's death had accidentally fallen into my lap, but just because it wasn't my first priority didn't mean I wouldn't see it through to the end. When it came to endings, I made sure I crossed the finish line once, if not two or three times.

Ty asked, "Have you got this thing wrapped up yet?"

"Just about," I said.

Evelyn ushered me inside, Ty closed the door, and I found the living room without any trouble. The paintings remained in place; Ty had on a different pair of loafers, a Polo shirt, and a pair of crisp, white pants; Evelyn had on a pair of red, three inch heels, a soft pink hat, her fashionable lenses, and a smooth, beige blouse.

"Are you stalling?" he asked.

"No, I just want to make sure I have my facts straight. I don't go around half-cocked, and the last time I checked, I still had my sanity."

"And who have you narrowed it down to?" Ty said.

"Bradley Cassidy and Veronica Sutton. Lana Ralstein still bothers me, but I don't think she chained a lead ball around my ankle, tossed me over the side of my rented boat, and made me hold my breath for two minutes."

"Just what kind of crazy mess are you involved in, son? Or should I even bother to ask?"

"You don't want to know," I said. "I manage to get myself in more trouble than a rock star in a hotel room. Lucky for me, though, I always land on all fours."

"If it's Veronica Sutton, do I get to pistol whip her?"

"Do you want to pistol whip her?"

"I always thought it might be kind of fun," he said. "And I could use the rush. The only thing that keeps me going these days is travel, the bedroom, tennis, and TV."

"You didn't have any other daughters?"

"Never got around to it," Ty said. "Life always got in the way. If you decide making babies is the thing for you, make sure you get all you can handle. Otherwise you might regret you didn't have more."

I shuddered at the thought. I couldn't even hold onto a girlfriend. "I'm pretty sure I'm a one-man operation."

"Don't ever give up hope," Evelyn said, "otherwise you'll never get it back."

Evelyn and Ty had a few more questions, and I just happened to have a few more answers. When I was through, I decided I should pay another visit to Frank and Jill Mason. I couldn't resist the opportunity to stuff Frank full of information and watch him blow up. I wanted a front row seat for the fireworks.

"Have you come here to put my mind at ease?" Frank asked. "Or are you here to watch Jeopardy?" In one motion, he shoved me inside and closed the door.

"I hope so. My mind is tired of going a hundred miles an hour. I might as well let some of the air out of my tires."

He said, "Is the finish line near at hand, or is it still a ways off?"

"Define near."

"Are you going to solve this case before Christmas," he said, "or do I need to get you a Santa Claus outfit?"

"What have the cops told you?" I said.

"The cops are idiots. I could outwit Rick and Adam with half of my brain cells fried. What do you have to do to get a badge around here? Subscribe to the Internet?"

"You have to pass a background check, a written exam—"

"Is the exam multiple choice?" Frank asked.

"Not when I took it," I said.

Jill watched me in her semi-passive state; the fake artwork watched me from a greater distance; Frank was on the edge of his seat, ready to pounce. I admired his passion. Only women and near-death experiences offered me the same provocation.

I told him what I knew, and then I sat back and waited. I started counting in my head, and before I reached six, Frank began again.

"If the old witch did it, I'm going to peel her lips off with a flamethrower."

I wasn't sure that was possible, but I smiled just the same. I showed myself out, while Frank popped a series of pills and then slammed them back with a glass of orange juice. I never did ask what the pills were.

The Hot Spot was the last spot on my list. Maybe I should've aimed higher, and maybe I should've ran faster, but I was more than ready to call it a day. I could attack Bradley Cassidy or Veronica Sutton when I had more information. I preferred it much more when I could ask a question that I already had the answer to, or at least had a good idea of what the answer would be. It didn't happen nearly as often as I would have liked it to; I didn't have sex nearly as often as I imagined; I didn't solve nearly enough cases to keep myself entertained. But I made do anyway.

The bar was semi-crowded; the band kicked off their set; the glasses were flowing; the women were plentiful; the L-shaped bar was half-filled; and I saw at least five women that I wouldn't have minded getting to know a little better.

"How dirty is your mind?" Dragon Lady asked.

I winked. "It's as dirty as you can get." I leaned in toward the bar, brushed the shoulder of a lean redhead, just as a Heineken plopped down in my general direction. I took a seat in the middle of the action and sat back to observe the party.

"So what can I do you out of?"

"That's my line," I said.

"I know. I'm giving you a taste of your own medicine. You need to swallow it whole and come back for seconds. Only then will I offer my words of wisdom."

"Now, why would you want to go and do a thing like that?" I said. "My life is surrounded by multiple opportunities, gorgeous women, and plenty of alcohol."

She did two beers at once, and then she did two more. I watched the first two spin into oblivion in one direction, and then I watched the other two spin in the other direction. I tried not to lose sight of my objective. Women were a thing of the past, present, and future, and I had all the time in the world.

She said, "Are you going to question me? Or are you going to leave your arguing to a minimum?"

"Should I?" I said. I took a long pull on my Heineken before I put it down.

"I wouldn't if I were you."

"Why's that?"

"Because you need me a lot more than I need you," Dragon Lady said.

She had three glasses lined up and a silver mixer at the edge of the bar. I watched as she threw in ice, poured contents from two light bottles, a dark bottle, and one fancy blue bottle, shook furiously, and then poured the liquid into the three glasses. She left me as I stared at my Heineken, the redhead next to me, the band behind me, and the mirror in front of me. I needed to ensure I covered all the bases.

When she returned, I said, "You know, that's the first time a woman has ever told me that. Maybe I should mark this occasion down in my diary."

"You don't have a diary," she said.

I opened my mouth, thought better of it, and then closed it right back up. The bottle of Heineken laughed at me or, at a minimum, took her side.

"And it won't be the last time either."

"Why?" I said. "Are you going to manipulate all the women I date? If you are, you might want to get started right away, since you're a bit behind the power curve."

"That would take a lifetime. What I am going to do is change your perception of reality. That won't take a considerable amount of time, and it will benefit society as a whole. If I can change you, I'll have made my mark on the world."

"If you can change me, you're better than anyone else I've ever met. And then they should name a city, state, street, and museum after you."

She said, "I am." Not the slightest hint of arrogance.

Dragon Lady filled more orders, dropped another Heineken in my lap, and left me to stare at the redhead a bit more, who happened to be here with her fiancé who stood about two inches taller than me and about forty pounds heavier—pure muscle. So, if I were to stand a chance against him, I'd need to hook him up to an IV and pump alcohol through his veins. He didn't seem particularly inclined to my intravenous tendencies, but I figured with a little prodding I could warm him up to the cause. His stare could have made the wind blow in the opposite direction.

Dragon Lady returned to me several moments later, minus the harsh stare, although her gaze did end this side of penetrating. It was more like a needle headed straight for my eye, and I wasn't about to back down.

"Besides my infinite wisdom, which we have discussed on multiple occasions, what did you want to talk about?" she asked.

With my Heineken and Dragon Lady as audience members, I laid out the details of the case in no particular order. "Well, Bradley Cassidy is more than just a sperm donor. Apparently, he, like Derrick Stevens and Kathryn Gable, was in love with Jessica Mason. Cindy

Bell's suicide is a no-go. There's still a slight chance she could have overdosed, but the odds are becoming less and less likely, and murder is becoming more and more likely.

"Lana Ralstein, my dancing partner, near as I can tell, wasn't the one to toss me overboard—"

"Wait," she said. "Back up a minute."

So, I told her about my dance lesson, the dip in the ocean and my subsequent conversation with Lana, the dark circles under her eyes, and the bandage on her forehead.

"Have you talked to both sets of parents?"

"I've kept them in the loop as much as I could. But there're still a few things I need to work out on my own. I have a hair sample I need to match to the saliva sample found on Jessica's body, and that should be about all she wrote."

"At least that's your hope," she said.

More drink orders were taken and filled, more people flocked into the bar (more women meant an equal number of men were likely to appear), and the band got louder. With the redhead out of sight, I began to look for a wider audience, before my eyes flicked back to Dragon Lady.

"How does one gain and maintain power?" I asked.

"Many of the world's leaders gained power by serving their own agendas and not caring about the consequences of their actions. And they remained in power because they'd do whatever it took to stay there. Even if it meant killing those underneath them."

"So their moral code flew right out the window?"

"No, they didn't have one to begin with. And absolute power made it even less likely that they might suddenly gain one."

"So people in a position of authority lack the most common moral values?"

"Some do," she said. "But they often have it on a higher scale, because power and corruption go together like lemons and water."

"I happen to have a slanted moral code myself."

She winked at me. "Whatever you tell yourself to get to sleep at night."

35

We were at Beverly Elmond's place, with her lace curtains, flower print sofa, and enough candles to start a large forest fire. If I needed to run, I was afforded that luxury. We hadn't gotten to the part where we were both naked—I was pretty sure that would come later. I'd have to smooth out a few feathers first.

My girlfriend of the moment had blond hair and a soft smile, when she wasn't using her eyes to stare at me like twin pinpricks of light from across the dining room table. I had a plate in front of me, but I was paying more attention to her than I was the plate. With a knife never far out of her reach, I was on amber alert threatening to go to fire-engine red. At the moment, we were talking about jobs and before that, what could have been the demise of our relationship, based on the amount of attention I had currently paid her.

"I don't have a real job, so I'm just going to mooch off of you." That was a lie. She owned her own business, a bakery. She couldn't cook worth crap, but she ran a mean business. In fact, she took care of everything but the cooking. She couldn't clean either.

"You still have the trust fund, right?"

"Yes, I do," I said. The stock market had gone on a steady climb and so had my trust fund. I didn't pick my own funds: I had a broker to do that sort of thing. He even managed to charge me on a per transaction basis: I was in the wrong business.

"You're not eating."

"I'm not hungry." Unless I was mistaken, my plate had moved a half-inch since I'd taken my seat; Beverly's knife had moved more than that.

"You're always hungry," she said. "I don't buy it. What's the real story?"

I thought for a minute. "Do you have enough money?"

"For what?" she asked. The puzzled look on her face was priceless. Her harsh look had managed to come down just a tad. I needed my video camera.

"To buy my love," I said. I drank a bit more Heineken, and then I maneuvered the food on my plate. The main course looked like fish: It might have been chicken. It might have been edible, or it might not. I shoved a piece of the concoction in my mouth just to be sure.

"Why would I want to do a thing like that?"

"It doesn't hurt to ask," I said. I'd been given the runaround by a lot of women—I was used to the abuse. Women would never get used to me: I was one of a kind and getting better with age.

"You're not going to get the answers you want," Beverly said.

I couldn't figure Beverly out, and I wasn't doing much better with Veronica and Lana. I didn't understand any of the women in my life right now, including Alexandra, my other girlfriend and a more exotic beauty. Beverly proved to be more classic in every sense of the word. I understood Ian, but he wasn't a woman, even though he acted like one. Maybe it was the job. Being a cop had gotten to me too. That's why I decided the heck with it, and I quit while I still had all of my hair and my good looks.

After a few bites, one of which had induced my gag reflex, I shoved my plate aside and shoved myself in the direction of her living room. Less than a heartbeat later, she followed suit, taking up residence beside me.

"It's the case, isn't it? That's the reason your attitude has changed."

I nodded.

"You can quit, you know."

"I know," I said. I didn't have it in me to quit. I could stick it out with the best of them, and I'd stick it out longer than the rest of them. All I needed was for the final two to become one, and then I could have my fun. If I could just get past the little matter of getting myself killed in the process.

"But you're not going to."

"No."

"Why not?" she asked. She'd moved closer to me, and I figured she might sit in my lap. She didn't. We'd moved away from her solid wood dining room table with feminine features. It made lap sitting a lot easier.

I preferred the bed, but I settled for the flower print sofa. I had my arm around her, and she had her hand resting on my thigh. It was a cute pose. We could have been the picture on a Hallmark greeting card.

"Because I see things through to the end," I said. "I'm going to figure this one out. I have two doors in front of me, and I'm going to make sure I pick the right one. When I do, I'll find out what I need to know."

"Maybe there are more than two doors," Beverly said.

"I've thought of that," I said. "There aren't. With any case, there're always a few pieces missing, and nothing is ever a sure thing, but if you get the ninety-five percent solution, you're doing all right." *Just as long as I don't end up ninety-five percent dead.*

"So you're going to pursue it anyway, despite the risks."

I'd told her about my near-death experience, and she wasn't happy about it. Frankly, I wasn't either. I still didn't know who had done the whacking. The demise of my gun proved troublesome as well.

"It's my job to fill in the blanks," I said. "I have two families counting on me, Kathryn Gable seeking answers, and Jessica Mason deserves justice."

I moved my hand lower, and she scooted away. This was a definite sign something was wrong. I could have asked her—I didn't figure it would do much good. If I gave her about five minutes, she'd tell me anyway. It ended up taking less than that.

"So how many other women are you seeing?" she asked.

"You don't like our arrangement?"

"A girl has to have attention," she said. "If she doesn't get it, she starts looking for it elsewhere."

I offered women the same line, and I served it on a silver platter.

"You're not giving me enough of your time."

"I wasn't aware you were looking for it elsewhere." I thought she only had eyes for me. Just because I wanted to increase my numbers didn't mean she had the right to.

"You never know when I might start."

"Is this your way of warning me?" I said. I didn't try to touch her chest this time. I occupied myself with rubbing her thigh instead. She didn't try to push my hand away. If she had, it wouldn't have mattered—I would have tried harder. I made a habit out of getting what I wanted.

"Someone has to."

"And you feel it's your duty."

"Among other things," Beverly said. There was a twinkle in her eye that hadn't been there a moment ago. The twinkle looked good on her. It would have looked even better if she'd been naked. "So do you plan on looking?" Her hand rubbed my crotch, so I lost track of what was going on. It was a good feeling, and I was willing to bet she did it on purpose. She could distract a minister giving his Sunday sermon.

She smiled. She always had a nice smile. I couldn't get away from it even if I wanted to. That was what attracted me first with women: their smiles. After the smile, it was the eyes, then the cheekbones, their teeth, and then my gaze started going south. For some strange reason, once my gaze started going lower it couldn't find its way back up. Once my eyes found a woman's chest, my radar was locked, loaded, and ready to fire.

She stood up, towering over me. Only a few women could tower over me in heels. I appreciated the rarities—homicides, beautiful women, and fast cars. Beautiful women, with more curves than a West Virginia highway, were the best rarity of all. I made sure I took the scenic route every chance I got.

She bent over and took my hand. When she did, she exposed her breasts. I did my best not to look—it didn't work.

"You haven't answered my question," I said.

"And you haven't answered mine." She started removing her clothes, and I couldn't remember what we were talking about, let alone what my question was. I decided losing track of my thoughts was for a good cause, so I went with it. In less than a minute she was as naked as a streaker on a soccer field, and she demanded to know why I hadn't taken off my clothes as well. Before I could think of a good answer, she started jerking at my top and bottom.

Twenty minutes later she was lying in my arms, and we were both having trouble breathing. She'd screwed the breath right out of me. I didn't know how long it would take me to get it back. If I started to go into shock, my only hope was that she was CPR certified; otherwise, I was a dead man.

I would have gotten out of bed if I thought I could move the lower half of my body. I spotted my clothes halfway across the room. Hers were even farther away. Out of the corner of my eye I peered at her nakedness—her skin was so white it was almost translucent. She had the body of a runner, which was ironic because she hated to run. I ran my slick fingers all over her naked body, and in a flash I was turned on all over again.

"Don't even think about it," she said. "You and I need to have a serious talk."

36

The next morning I had just reached my desk when my door burst open. When my door clanged open unannounced, more often than not, I wasn't happy with who stepped through. This time was no exception. Mayberry and Stephens stood side by side, shoulder to shoulder, in matching shirts.

"Do you guys ever sleep?" I asked.

"Do you ever shut up?"

"My mouth has its own state, and it's the size of Texas." My coffee maker stopped dripping, and I poured myself a cup. I didn't offer any refreshments to my new roommates since I wanted them gone as soon as possible. "Are you two in an information-sharing mode?"

"We're in a whack-you-over-the-head-with-a-shovel mode," Stephens said.

"I didn't see that one in the manual," I said. "I'm not even sure it's legal. Are you sure you know what you're doing, or are you just pretending?"

Mayberry ignored my last comment. "Neither are some of your methods. We're even."

"Now, we're getting into semantics," I said. "It's easy to get lost in the details and end up flat on your face."

"I knew we should have left you in jail. You're a menace to society."

"I'm not the kind of guy who likes to be tied down. You'd need a bigger rope than either of you could ever find."

"We've heard," Mayberry said.

"You mean my reputation precedes me? I'd rather bask in all of its infinite glory. That way I keep my head at a reasonable level."

"Your reputation is all you've got. You're a former cop who couldn't cut it in the cop world. You're so far away from reality you have no hope of ever returning."

"I had trouble respecting authority," I said. "It's always the minor details that get you. And you never know when they're going to rear their ugly little heads."

Mayberry said, "You have trouble following rules. And our one rule was for you to let this one rest. And you couldn't even follow that advice. Your simple mind just got even simpler. And our lives just got infinitely more complicated because of you."

"Once I start something, I don't quit," I said. "I see it through all the way to the end, no matter where the road takes me or who I have to step on to get there."

"You're giving us migraines," Mayberry said. "Our tolerance level just hit a new low, and it's threatened to go even lower."

"I'm glad I'm leveling the playing field. I wouldn't want you two to end up on easy street, and then I'm the one who finds every speed bump."

"There is no field left for you," Mayberry said. "You're on the bench, and you're trying to throw yourself into the game. The coach had to drag you by the uniform and toss you back behind the sideline."

Mayberry and Stephens had matching glares.

I had my second cup of coffee in front of me, and I wanted to down it as quickly as possible, just in case this was my last meal and the two nitwits decided to do something rash. I could handle jail, and I could handle two individuals with the combined IQ of a hummingbird, but I wasn't sure I could handle both at the same time without my morning dose of caffeine.

"Not only is the present in jeopardy," Mayberry said, "but you're drudging up the past as well. We're going to need a backhoe to clean up the mess you've made."

"I'm a rather curious individual," I said. "I can't say no to a good time. And having the two of you and your sunny personalities walk through my door is the closest I've gotten to a party in just over a week. I'd have had streamers ready, but the party supply store doesn't open for another hour."

Mayberry ignored me. "And our warnings?"

"What warnings?" I said. "Did I miss another memo? I told you to send them via snail mail, since I don't check my email on a regular basis, and as you can see I don't have a fax machine handy. I use the local OfficeMax for all my faxing needs."

Stephens leaned over my desk, bracing his weight with his left hand, and punched me in the gut, his face only a few inches from my own.

Mayberry watched with a smirk on his face.

Since my abs are toned to perfection, the two blows felt like bee stings. All of my sit-ups had better come in handy, or I would have to ask for a refund.

Stephens shifted his position away. "You're invading my space so much I'm getting claustrophobic."

"I never did fear enclosed spaces," I said. "They give me a new perspective."

With my second cup of coffee finished, I leaned back in my chair, closed my eyes, and considered going to sleep.

A hand reached out toward me, and I caught it in mid-air.

"The touching needs to stop," I said. "I'm no longer amused."

Mayberry said, "So do you have all the answers, wise guy?"

"Most of them. I still have one or two theories to run down, but I should be finished later on today. If not, should be first thing tomorrow. I'd rather not leave any loose ends dangling around. How are you guys doing?"

"It's a dead case," Stephens said.

"I thought it was a dead body."

Mayberry said, "There's that, too."

I ran a hand through my hair. The glares turned a new shade of hostile; I didn't wither under the heat lamp.

"You guys never really learn, do you?" I said.

"Do you think your friend Ian learns?" Stephens asked.

"He's a helpful individual."

"He could also be stuck as a detective for a really long time," Mayberry said. His hands had never left his pockets.

"I don't really think he cares," I said.

"Some kind of misguided loyalty shit," Stephens said.

"Yeah, something like that. My friends don't sell their souls to the devil for a glazed doughnut."

"And you're going to continue to feed him," Mayberry said.

"If I have to," I said, "yeah. He helps me through some trouble spots, and I help him find the trouble areas, so we tend to balance each other out."

"You two deserve each other," Stephens said.

"We most certainly do."

Stephens and Mayberry turned 180 degrees and walked out through the door the exact way they had come in. I watched them go, and then my thoughts drifted to the glazed doughnut. I didn't need the sugar rush: It might tempt me to do bad things.

I considered throwing darts at a dartboard to solve my case, but I didn't have darts and I didn't have a dartboard, so I dropped that theory like a nice pair of pink lace underwear. I had the underwear image in full bloom when my phone rang.

"I have your sample analyzed," Isabel Titler said.

"Am I going to like the results?"

"Probably," she said. "It's Bradley Cassidy."

"Oh, goody," I said. "I didn't need a new suspect. I like it much better when I can work with the ones I've got. Makes things simpler that way." I pitched an imaginary dart at an imaginary spot on the wall.

"So do I get my reward?" she asked.

"What kind of reward do you want? If you're looking for a genie, you've been greatly misguided. In fact, I'd probably ask for a full-out refund."

"The sparkly kind," she said.

"I was thinking more along the lines of the sweaty kind, myself. I might even be able to drum up a whip, handcuffs, tight leather outfit, and lace panties."

"Euuwww," she said. "I need to hose myself down."

I lost some stiffness from the nether regions.

That's the first time a woman had ever told me that, and I knew it wouldn't be the last. Strange world. And it kept getting stranger. I wondered if alien life forms were in the foreseeable future.

"Well, before you start the water," I said, "I need to know how hard it is to make a murder look like a suicide."

"You were a cop," Isabel said. "You should know . . . unless you went brain dead sometime in the last seven minutes. All you need is the right prescription, and the killer just points the cops where he wants them to go. If you can think like a cop, you can certainly fool a cop."

"You make it sound so simple."

"Casey, most things in life are. And then there's you. You need your own instruction manual and deciphering key."

And then the line went dead.

My Viper was available, and I had a new set of questions to ask, so I decided to dig up some answers before the alien life forms came to take over. The dance studio was on my mind, and more specifically, Bradley Cassidy. I found him in the smallest of the three rehearsal rooms with a new headband and a new attitude that needed a bit of work.

"If you yank another hair off my head," he said, "I'm going to take a baseball bat to your skull."

"You could certainly try," I said. "However, your odds of success are only about fifty-fifty. And depending on your skill with a bat, they might be closer to forty-sixty or thirty-seventy."

"I don't have to try," he said. "All I need is the will to take you down."

"I didn't know your hair was so sensitive. Maybe I should issue it a formal apology. All I need is the proper paperwork and the right tone of voice." I had one hand on the wall and the other was in my pocket.

Bradley had both hands in front of him, ready for action.

"Do you mind explaining to me what your watch and saliva were doing on Jessica Mason's body?"

He ignored my question. "Am I going to need a lawyer?"

"I hope not," I said. "I don't really like dealing with lawyers. Besides, I'm not the police. And I'm not going to take you in for questioning, I just want to know what's really going on around here."

"But you could turn me over to them."

"That's true," I said. "I could make a citizen's arrest. But I don't have any handcuffs, and my pistol is in the car." *Actually, it was at the bottom of the ocean, or so I thought.*

"Are you that kind of citizen?"

"I might be," I said. "Can you tell me where you were the night Jessica Mason died?"

"I was in Florida," Bradley said. "Orlando, to be exact."

"Can you prove it?"

"I can. I have my airline ticket, and I might still have my baggage receipt."

"Shit," I said. "That's not the kind of news I was looking for."

"What?"

"That means I have to cross you off my list."

Bradley shook his head. His headband stood in place during the head movement. "You've gotta be the craziest PI I've ever met."

I leaned even harder on the wall. "Have you met any others?"

"No," he said. His hands had dropped to his side, and he no longer appeared as tense as a female during a horror movie.

"Good," I said. "That means I've tainted you for all time."

The rehearsal room was empty—except for us—the music was soft, almost to the point of being non-existent, and he had done a series of stretches, splits, and other various limber movements that made me want to grab my nuts. I kept my hands in my pockets in case they decided to get minds of their own.

"Do you know why someone would plant your hair and watch?"

"I'm an easy scapegoat," he said. "I'm the crazy father to an unborn child, I loved her, and I'm also a colleague."

Those were my sentiments exactly. "But you don't seem like a complete psychopath, and you have an alibi. And you're one of the saner people I've met around here."

"Maybe the real killer didn't know that," he said. "The average criminal isn't a scientist with a Ph.D."

"Just what are you trying to say?"

"It was a short notice trip," he said. "My grandfather died. I went down to pay my respects. I bought my ticket at the airport, and I paid in cash."

I didn't bother to ask where he had gotten that kind of cash. I didn't have time for another investigation. And my expertise wasn't in the financial arena.

I did, however, have some respects I'd like to pay. And I'd need a big wallet.

37

Without my consent or knowledge, my Viper headed in the general direction of Gloria Headwitz, with her laissez faire attitude and connection to Cindy Bell, and there wasn't a thing I could do to stop it. Not that I was concerned, I was more along the lines of intrigued, and I was infinitely closer to curious. The purple and pink panties, the full-length mirrors on the walls and ceiling, and the sultry, sexy voice did that to me.

Even though I had yet to find the video cameras, I could feel their presence, and I did feel a slight twinge of excitement. For the sake of the case, I had to ensure both she and I kept our clothes on; otherwise, I might end up in the middle of a firing squad with my pants around my ankles. Or she might pursue the handcuffs, tight leather, and lace underwear combination. I wasn't sure I had enough willpower to resist an all-out assault.

"What are you doing back here?" she asked.

"I'm just tying up a few loose ends. I'd like to get my account settled today, and I'd prefer one without a residual balance."

"I don't suppose you'd let me tie you up, would you? I even have a leather outfit, fuzzy handcuffs, and lace underwear."

I had a perfect visual of her lace panties. I also noticed a nude portrait of her at the other end of her living room. I'd missed it last time.

"Are you going to untie me later?"

"Probably not," she said. "Especially if you're going to get pushy about it. I'll even make sure you get naked and stay naked."

"Are you always this forward? Or do I get the special PI treatment package?"

"Don't pretend you don't enjoy it," Gloria said. "You wouldn't know what to do with yourself if you didn't have a woman hitting on you six or seven times a day."

"I saw pink panties in your sofa the last time; I caught a glimpse of your purple underwear before; this time you have on a pale blue number. I could arrest you for aggravated assault, and you'd have to shimmy and shake your way out of that one."

"I like to let you know what you're getting yourself into," she said. "By the way, have you seen my strobe light and long pole?"

I considered asking her whether or not she was serious. I leaned toward the affirmative, so I decided it was better not to go down that road. I only had four condoms in my pocket, and that wasn't near enough protection.

"I've seen bulls less forward than you."

"I'm just trying to get you naked," she said. "I have an objective and a plan, and I'm sticking to it. No need to make things more complicated."

I said, "You're not the first woman, and you certainly won't be the last."

She headed for the kitchen as I tried to decide if all three mirrors had cameras, or just two of them. It was a tough call, and it'd be extremely difficult to get visual confirmation. I assumed the swinging chandelier could hold her weight and possibly even mine. I'd never done it in the air before, although I figured it was worth doing before I had a headstone named after me.

She touched the glass to her lips and took a large swallow. I watched her throat muscles work, and I hoped they weren't as strong as they looked.

"Are you under some sort of deadline?" she asked.

"It's of my own creation," I said. "I have to be on vacation in the next two days, or I'm liable to end up with my hair on fire and my pants around my knees—and choking on seaweed."

She almost choked on her drink. "And why is that?"

"Because this whole case is one giant bomb, and eventually the fuse is going to run out, and I don't want to be in the kitchen when the whole thing explodes. I want to dart out the door, say goodbye to my appliances, and never look back."

"You definitely have a way with words."

"I try to choose them carefully," I said, "and I'm a pretty good listener."

She nodded, downed more of her beverage of choice, and then leaned forward. "So what have you found out?"

"Well, I'm pretty sure Veronica Sutton committed both murders. Bradley Cassidy wasn't around fourteen years ago, and he has an alibi for Jessica. But the killer did a real good job of framing him, except for the simple fact that she didn't check with the airlines to verify he was around. Otherwise, he would have made the perfect scapegoat: He was the father of Jessica's unborn child; he had to fend off not one extra suitor but two; he was in love with her—and love and hate go together about as well as lettuce and tomato—and he was her colleague. He also happens to be in good shape."

Gloria told me she hated Veronica with a passion best reserved for other activities, right before she downed the rest of her beverage, and then went back for another.

I wondered if I should take advantage of her. But even if her eyes rolled back in her head, I had the feeling she would still be taking advantage of me.

Gloria returned, drink in hand. This drink was as steady as the first one. "Was there ever any doubt?"

"You had an idea this whole time?" I said. "And you didn't share it with me? Just what kind of friend are you?"

"I had a hunch," she said. "And you just confirmed my suspicions. You're a smart man, governor. Smarter than any of the cops ever were.

Maybe she kept her panties in check when the cops were around. Or then again, maybe she didn't. "Smart enough to connect the dots," I said. "And that's not really saying much. I still can't believe you didn't offer me any help. I could have died out at sea."

"Are you the kind of person that asks for help on a regular basis?"

"Not exactly," I said. "I try to limit my cries for assistance."

"I'm not either."

38

"Ian, you're a pain in the neck," I said. I couldn't think of a better way to start out my conversation with my best friend. He hadn't put me in any difficult positions; however, I'd managed to put him in a few over the years. I'd dialed his number, and he'd picked up on the second ring, a model of efficiency.

"But it's a good pain."

"No pain is good pain," I said. I should know. I'd been in all kinds of pain. I'd been the recent recipient of a trip to the bottom of the ocean, and my handgun went along for the ride. I'd found a replacement and had it stashed in my glove compartment, just in case any loonies tried to hijack my Viper. I'd also filed a report on my missing firearm just in case it sprung back to life in the middle of winter.

"So you're the expert now?"

"I'm an expert in everything."

There was a pause on Ian's end. I knew he was trying to think of some witty comeback. He didn't have as many as I did. And if he did have wit, he probably used most of it up on me. He had a short supply, and his supply had gotten even shorter in the time I knew him.

I just shook my head. I'd been baffled a lot the past few days, and my bafflement was running out of steam. It needed a new life, and I wasn't sure how many embers I had left to keep the flame burning. Even if my mind wasn't going full speed ahead, it moved at a gallop. If I wasn't careful, I'd come to a standstill, and then I'd trip over my own two feet.

I was back in my office with my feet up on my desk, a cup of coffee in front of me, day six of the Jessica Mason murder—or day eight, since it took Kathryn Gable two days to track me down—and my distraction named Mandy Humphrey across the hall. We'd already exchanged smiles once this morning, and I held out hope for a second round. I would have taken her clothes as well: My wardrobe could use a new spark of life.

"I'm still trying to figure out why you called me," Ian said.

"Isn't it painfully obvious?" I said.

"Nothing with you is ever painfully obvious. You seem to cause yourself a lot of pain, and others around you get sucked in as well. I'm trying to figure out how you find every black void imaginable. You like to leave me in the dark until the lack of nothingness takes over and sweeps me under."

Ian is always a little too dramatic and a bit too much of a pessimist. It makes for a deadly combination, and I've found the best way to handle him is to ignore his jabs. If I swat at him, he just comes back for seconds.

"I learned how to dance; I solved two murders for the price of one—"

"You didn't learn how to do anything," he said. "All you did was postpone death for another day. Sooner or later it will catch up with you. I'm not sure how much longer you can dance with the devil and live to tell the tale. If you want to survive, you're going to need a bigger set of horns."

"That's what I need your help on," I said. "I knew you were good for something, you could always jar the truth right out of me. Even though you hit like a girl and you're skinny enough to hula-hoop through a Cheerio, you always lead me down the right road. If it weren't for you, I'd probably get lost more often, and one of these days I wouldn't find my way back."

"You better watch those images. I know how your imagination gets carried away. It's liable to lift you up by the seat of your pants and drop you on your head."

"It's all in the name of fun," I said.

"You and I have different definitions of fun."

"That's because you don't have one," I said. "Fun isn't some three letter word you look up in the dictionary. You have to go out and experience it."

"You mentioned death."

"I did."

"You're not going to kill yourself, are you? Because if you are, I want to give your eulogy. I figure I'm the only one qualified enough to last more than three minutes without taking all of my clothes off."

"I hadn't planned on it," I said. "But I need to talk with Veronica Sutton, and I'm going to need backup because she's going to be more than a little pissed after I'm through with her. She might try to slug me or put a slug through my heart. I don't hit women, at least not intentionally, and even though my heart may not always function the way it should, I happen to like it very much."

"Isn't that a little out of my job description? I thought I was just the research guy. Besides, I'm too skinny to throw a punch. You're going to need protection in the form of a pump-action shotgun. And even that might not be enough."

He had the same job description every time—he just liked to give me a hard time about his duties. Ian probably couldn't sleep well at night if he didn't put up a fuss every step of the way. I didn't always pay attention, and he didn't always know the difference, so I figured we were even.

"You don't have to throw a punch. All you have to do is come to my rescue," I said. "And you can even call in some of your buddies, if you want. In fact, I'd recommend it. Just avoid Mayberry and Stephens. They might try to gun me down in the ensuing melee."

"What do I have to do?"

"I need wired up, suited up, and when I give you the sign, you need to call in the cavalry. I don't sacrifice myself unless it's for a good cause."

"And how are you going to get yourself in this jam?"

"By walking right up to the enemy and getting a good old-fashioned confession," I said. "I'm pretty sure they're still legal in all fifty states and the District of Columbia. And, no, I'm not going to give you all the details. That way, if my plan backfires, you can plead ignorance. If I'm going down, I don't want to take you with me. You still have a wife who loves you and a job that pays just enough for you to retire some day."

Ian groaned. "You haven't done a day of old-fashioned detective work in your life. Death is your flotation device. And your chivalrous leanings leave me with an icky sensation in the pit of my stomach. Too much lemon meringue pie has the same effect."

"That's your opinion."

"And I'm sticking to it," Ian said.

Did I mention he could be a little stubborn? On the other hand, so could I.

"When are you going to get yourself in this jam?"

"As soon as possible," I said. "Definitely tonight. I'd like to beat my deadline with time to spare. That way I have an extra day to soak up the rays, the beach bunnies, the string bikinis, and the spray-on tans. Life doesn't get much better than that."

"What the hell am I supposed to tell Nicola?" Ian asked. He didn't make a habit out of cussing, so I was surprised he had taken the time to do it. In fact, I almost dropped my coffee cup.

"This is the night I'm supposed to get lucky. You're going to spoil my fun."

Nicola, Ian's wife for much longer than a moment, never faltered in her love for the straight man.

"That's pathetic," I said. "Just tell her you're doing me a favor. And make sure you get a rain check. I wouldn't want you to have to wait a whole month before you get lucky again."

"Yeah, like that will go over real well. She probably won't speak to me for a week." I let him rant. "And if I don't do it?"

He didn't complain very loudly, so I was pretty sure I had him. I just had to wear him down a bit more. If I had one strong suit, it was my ability to use my mouth to my advantage. Of course, if I wasn't careful, it tended to get me in a bit of trouble as well.

I said, "I could always hunt you down and kick your butt."

"Flattery will get you nowhere."

I paused and considered my choices. I didn't have a dartboard handy to pick my next course of action. "I'll owe you a favor."

"Anything I want?" Ian asked.

"Sure."

He didn't answer right away, so I knew it was going to be something I didn't want to do. But Ian had helped me out of more jams than I could count, even if he did tell me about every last one of them later. Deep down he was a good guy, probably a better guy than I was. I wasn't going to tell him that. I didn't want his head to swell up to the size of a watermelon.

"All right, I'll do it," Ian said. He still hadn't told me what he wanted—I was pretty sure I'd get the bill later.

39

After I got off the phone with Ian, I decided to visit him at the Virginia Beach PD so I could get suited up. I strutted into the station like a peacock on steroids. I didn't miss that hustle and bustle for a second. I preferred the calm.

The station hadn't changed much since I'd left. The rows of desks were in perfect alignment, the desks were about thirty paces deep, phones rang off the hook, approximately half the desks were filled, keys pounded in perfect unison, and the women appeared more butch than the have-a-good-time look I tended to prefer. A man dressed as a woman tried to proposition me, but I avoided his, or her, advances.

I found Ian in the middle of all the action. He had a wire handy, and I'd brought my own sport coat. He tested the device, told me it had a three-hour battery life, showed me where the on/off switch was located, told me he had a team on standby, and then he sent me on my way.

I hopped back in my Viper, pointed the car in the direction of the studio, and fought with the traffic on autopilot. I didn't have a shotgun handy, but I had a pistol in the glove compartment: a newer model than the previous one, semi-automatic with nine-millimeter shells.

I found Lana Ralstein in the first dressing room wearing nothing but a matching bra and panties.

"Do you know how to knock?" she asked.

"It covers up the same as a bikini," I said. "In fact, I'm willing to bet the bikini has less fabric than your current attire."

She shoved me outside and slammed the door.

I drummed my fingers on the door as I waited, and I smiled at the three women I saw while I held the door in place from the opposite side.

When she opened the door she had on a dark top, dark tights, and her long hair pulled up in a bun. She breezed right past me without saying a word. Since I needed to talk with her, I decided I should bring up the rear and put myself in perfect position to view her rear.

I decided blunt was the best way to deal with Lana Ralstein. "How are you involved in this whole mess?"

By tracking her down at the studio, I figured there were plenty of witnesses handy, just in case she lacked a certain amount of trustworthiness. I was almost 100 percent sure she didn't knock me over the head, chain my ankle, toss me over the side of my rented boat, and watch me drown, but all I could remember about the incident was a blunt object to the head, total darkness, and then I was surrounded by water, fighting for my life. And if I hadn't beaten the chain, the chain would've beaten me.

"I'm not." She'd found an empty rehearsal room and was in the process of limbering up. I took my shoes off and stepped inside before she changed her mind and tried to slam the door in my face. I had a better chance of keeping the conversation moving if I was on the other side of the door. I, however, didn't have a rhythmic or limber bone in my body. So I held up the door with one hand and stared at her limberness with both eyes, just in case her tights split right across her rear end.

"Then why did you abandon me?"

"I didn't abandon you," she said. "Did you see the bruise on my forehead? Like you, I was knocked unconscious, only I wasn't tossed over the side of the boat. When I came to, there was no one around, and I didn't realize until later that you had been dropped to the bottom of the ocean. You may lack rhythm, but that's no reason to try to cause your demise."

"Then why did you stop talking to me?"

"As I recall, you stopped talking to me," she said. She held her head up high in an act of defiance, and then she went right into a back bend. Lana was still a good seven inches shorter than me, but her back bent at more than twice the angle mine ever would.

"Because I thought you had something to do with my accident," I said. "It seemed rather convenient that you weren't around when I broke through the surface, and you disappeared right around the time I took one on the head. I never got a good view of my attacker. I saw black, and then I saw nothing at all."

"But I didn't."

"It's easier to see that now," I said. "You came away unscathed—"

"I had a bandage on my forehead and dark circles under my eyes. I'd hardly call that unscathed."

I nodded. "I probably have a few screws loose just for being here since I'm fairly certain Veronica Sutton either knocked off Jessica Mason and Cindy Bell, or she had help. However, I work much better when I fly with my underwear flapping in the breeze and do a cannonball right into the middle of the ocean. If I don't hang myself upside down once in a while, I'm missing out on a good part of the action. I'm just thankful I do enough sit-ups to pull myself back up."

"You still have your suspicions?"

"It's hard not to," I said. "You always have to worry about the pretty ones. And you're a lot smarter than you deserve to be. I still haven't figured out the motivation for your constant distractions. You are indeed one serious distraction. You in a string bikini should be outlawed in forty-six states."

Lana smiled out of the side of her mouth. "I could help you forget them. I could help you forget anything worth forgetting."

I didn't doubt her for a second, but I couldn't risk a distraction right now when the end was in sight.

She had stopped contorting her body into a human pretzel and took two giant steps toward me. Since I couldn't back up—otherwise I'd end up in the hallway and she might shut the door in my face—I stood like a sentry as I waited to see what she did next. I didn't have to wait long.

She kissed me long and hard and good.

I stopped her before she got too carried away. I wasn't sure where the gentleman in me came from—he didn't come around too often. I still didn't know what she was up to, and I still wasn't sure I could completely trust her.

"You could have saved me," I said.

"Not likely. From what I know about you, you have a hard enough time saving yourself. I would have just gotten in the way, and I had my own issues to deal with. I was glad to see you made it out alive."

"I'm pretty good at getting myself out of situations," I said. "And I'm rather adept at getting myself into tight spots as well. Trouble seeks me out the way a little kid seeks out a cookie jar."

With the end close at hand, I could take another vacation. I wasn't sure where I would go this time. I thought somewhere out of the U.S. might be nice; I might never bother to come back. The IRS could try to track me down. I didn't think they would have much luck, especially if I went somewhere like Brazil and hid out in the jungles. Or I could head to Africa and join a tribe. Or I could take a trip to Russia. I was pretty sure I'd fit right in with my blond hair. And many of the Russian women were downright stunning. I'd have to work on my ability to adapt to cold weather: I figured I was up for the challenge.

She huddled closer to me. "I was scared. Not just for myself, but for you."

I wasn't sure I believed her. I'd heard a lot of crap over the past few days, and I had trouble wading through all the muck. There were too many lies around me, and each lie seemed to lead to another one, like clues. Or cockroaches. Only clues helped me solve crimes. I wasn't going to solve anything by listening to cockroaches.

Lana wrapped her arms around herself and squeezed. She didn't squeeze tight enough because she wasn't gasping for breath. The stirring in my loins stopped, and I wasn't sure I wanted to bring it back.

Her kiss lingered on my lips, and I couldn't seem to dismiss it. I found her a whole lot sexier than I should have, and I couldn't do a thing about it.

"I thought I could trust you," I said.

"You still can."

I shook my head. "I'll still have the lagging doubts, no matter how much I try to get rid of them. You're more dangerous than you realize."

"I thought you and I had something," Lana said. I saw a bit of hurt in her eyes before it vanished. "But I guess I was wrong."

"I thought we did too," I said. And then I walked out. It was a lot harder than I thought it would be, and I wasn't quite sure why I just walked away. I had my pride, or what was left of it, and I had my thoughts, which continued to nag at me. I couldn't seem to put the two of them together, or if I could, there were still a few pieces missing.

I wasn't quite sure what lucky meant anymore.

I turned around and bumped right into Veronica Sutton. "You should listen to her," she said. "Lana did what she could to save your worthless behind. How do you think she ended up with the bandage on her forehead?"

"Maybe she put it there for decoration," I said.

She'd gone for the minimalist makeup look, which suited her just fine, even with her sharp pinched-like features and worry lines on her forehead. Despite being older, her attractiveness wasn't lost on me, and her toned legs didn't hurt either.

"Men are all the same. They think with the wrong head ninety-eight percent of the time. And yours is causing you to doubt what you should have accepted as fact a long time ago."

"Most of the time my instincts never fail me."

"The key words in that sentence are *most of the time*. You should work on being less of a screw up."

"I hear the local police department is recruiting these days," I said. "Have you ever thought about suiting up?"

"Have you ever thought about being less of a nuisance?"

I turned away from her, flicked the wire on with my left hand, and then I turned back around.

"What do you think you're doing?" Veronica asked.

"I have an itch. You're welcome to scratch it for me if you want. It's right between my legs, and it's getting bigger. Make sure you watch out for large objects."

In one motion, she whipped a black revolver out of her handbag and cracked me over the head. I didn't see it coming, and before I could process what had just happened, I saw stars, stripes, and a brief white light.

40

I came to in the back of a car with leather seats, leather trim, and one pissed off woman behind the wheel. My hands were tied, my head still had a slight ache, and the bumps jarred me around like a wooden roller-coaster.

"I get carsick on trips," I said. It was a small lie. Veronica wouldn't know the difference, and if I could break her, I might buy myself a little time. I didn't like to lie, but this was a situation where I deemed it was necessary. It had to do with the gun Veronica still had peeking out of her purse. Being shot once by some crazed drug addict missing a tooth was enough—I didn't need a repeat performance.

"Am I supposed to care?" she asked.

"I wouldn't want to throw up all over your car," I said.

Veronica made a small noise, and then she gagged while she drove with one hand and covered her mouth with the other.

"It's a rental," she said. "As long as I take it back in one piece, no one will know the difference." She smirked. "And you'll be long gone by then."

I couldn't think of a witty comeback. Being kidnapped sucked the wind right out of my sails, and it's a pretty big straw. A punch in the gut had the same effect. A large gun pointed in my direction didn't do me any favors either. At least the gun was in her handbag instead of pointed at my skull.

My thoughts drifted to Kathryn Gable: I never got to tell her what happened . . .

I struggled against the bindings, but they didn't give an inch. Maybe I should have let Ian plant the tracking device in my shoe. I could save myself a bit trouble, and I wouldn't have to worry about him getting lost in his attempted rescue. As it was, I needed a new plan, and I needed it fast.

"You can struggle all you want," she said. "They are made of plastic, and I secured them myself, so you're out of luck."

I said, "So where are we going?"

No reply.

I didn't like it when my questions went unanswered. I interrogated people for a living, and I felt I deserved a little respect. We hopped on I-264 going eastbound in the direction of the ocean.

"Is it some place dark and dreary? Does it have big walls, and are there shotgun shells all over the floor? How big is your gun, Veronica? I'd hate to think I was kidnapped by some half-wit who doesn't have the sense to carry a decent weapon. At the very least, you could do me the courtesy of carrying a semi-automatic. Revolvers went out of style fifty years ago. That way, if I try to run, you can pump my guts full of lead. Hey, I think I saw that in a movie once." I paused. "Yep, I'm sure I did. I can't remember the name of the movie. Did it have Arnold Schwarzenegger in it?"

"Goddamn it," she said, "I can't hear myself think." Her voice was louder than it should have been. That was a good sign. Maybe I had rattled her, or at the very least, thrown her off course. Now, if I could just think of an escape route where I didn't have to eject myself from a car moving at sixty-five miles an hour, I'd be home free.

"You actually have a coherent thought?" I said. "Do you have a plan, too? Why don't you stop the car right now and let me go? I can tell them I was lost, and you can save yourself some jail time. Killing two dancers puts you in a bit of trouble, obviously, but you might be able to work out a deal with a lenient DA and judge. However, kidnapping and pre-meditated murder puts you in a whole new category of psycho-crazy. You might have to spend your remaining days in a maximum security prison waiting for them to stick the needle in your vein."

"I have a plan," she said. "If you don't shut up, I'm going to mess up that pretty face of yours. No lady within a hundred miles will want to touch you. You'll have to start paying to get laid." The smirk was back, and it was even uglier.

I could almost hear the crashing waves and practically see the string bikinis lined up along the shoreline.

I turned around to look at the road behind us. I didn't see anything of interest other than a sea of cars, a set of flashing lights, a concrete barrier on the right side of the road, and my own impending doom. Darkness had just started to set in. I was used to the night. And I was used to getting myself into as well as out of tricky situations.

I squirmed in the back seat. My bladder had started filling up, and I didn't think I'd win any extra points by peeing all over the leather. I stared straight ahead as she exited the highway and then turned back toward the studio.

"Are you taking me back to the studio?" I asked. "Isn't this plan a bit convoluted? If you wanted to kill me, you could have saved yourself a lot of trouble by not tossing me in the car first."

"What's it to you?" Veronica asked. There was an edge to her voice. She wanted to sound a lot tougher than she really was.

"I want to know where I'm going to die."

"So you can pray for forgiveness?" she asked.

"Something like that." I wanted to know what my options of escape were. And I wanted a little time to work out this new and improved plan. I probably wouldn't get a chance to do either. It didn't hurt to hope.

I thought about Jessica's death. She'd been killed elsewhere, and then she'd been dumped in the dance studio parking lot. I began to see a bit of a pattern, and I didn't like it. And the rental car would be much harder to trace. She could take it back to Hertz or Enterprise or wherever she had gotten it. They'd have it cleaned up and ready for the next customer in no time. It was harder to trace than your own automobile; however, it wasn't in the same category as stealing a car. But if she didn't want to hold someone at gunpoint, and if she didn't know how to hot wire a car, this was a much better, and in most cases, a cleaner alternative. I still wasn't sure how friendly it was to the environment.

"So why did you do it? I realize you have your cardinal rule that the show must go on, and I realize sudden pregnancies put you in a bit of a bind, but there are better ways to handle your problems than to just start knocking people off. Maybe you should attend some anger management classes. I hear they're rather common at the YMCA these days, and you might get a special discount seeing as how you're a psycho and all."

Instead of answering questions, she concentrated on driving. Considering the way she used her horn, changed lanes, and jerked me all over the backseat, I was happy her eyes didn't leave the road. I just wondered how much more it would take to get her rattled again.

"Maybe you wanted them to leave on your terms, not theirs, and you just couldn't stand the thought of a lowly dancer getting the better of you. Have you ever heard of Waco? Cults are rather overrated these days. Individuals deserve the chance to think for themselves without being brainwashed by some former dancer who now has to satisfy herself with owning her own business."

"You should ask for forgiveness for all the sins you have committed," Veronica said, "and you are going to commit. It might make death a little easier to swallow."

"I have no problem with the gravity of death. I've almost drowned, been shot, hurled at a moving train, and almost plummeted to my death from the top of The Hot Spot, which just happens to be under new ownership, by the way. And they have an excellent selection to choose from, including the beers." I focused on the regulars who frequented the bar, and many of them just happened to be good looking women. It didn't work. "I'm not sure you can be forgiven for committing three murders."

She stopped at a red light, and I saw Walkman Theatre, the theatre space the Virginia Dance Company rented, peeking above a couple of restaurants, the Bank of Virginia, and a couple of local coffee shops. The theatre stared back at me in all its old-style neon glory.

"So what are you going to do with me?"

"I'm going to hang you over the catwalk and watch you die."

"At the theatre space you rent?" I said. "Are you sure that's a smart move?"

"We're not the only ones who use that space. And our performances don't start for another week and a half. I'm sure someone will find you in the meantime. I hear there's a Shakespearean play, two movies, and a local concert to help you pass the time."

I didn't like the joke. "You're actually threatening me?" I asked. "How are you going to get me up there all by yourself?"

"I have help," she said.

Maybe she had her own hired goons. I heard they were in style these days. I could have used three bodyguards, but none of them would have been able to keep up with me. I had a hard enough time keeping up with myself.

Veronica yanked the door open and shoved me outside. She pushed and cajoled me toward the theatre space and my impending doom. I just hoped I had the chance to say a few final prayers before I was forced to meet my maker. I figured it would probably take him about seven years to go over my list of transgressions.

"What are you smirking at?" she said.

"I was just thinking how much fun it would be to kick your ass."

Veronica just shook her head—right before she punched me in the gut. I was prepared for it, and my abs of steel deflected her punch. Five hundred sit-ups a day did wonders for my body. I watched as her face contorted in anger, and then she tried again. No such luck this time either. It just wasn't her lucky day.

I, however, still planned on having one of the luckiest days of my life.

Upon entrance into the theatre, I met her help: steroid-man. He stood approximately three inches taller than me, outweighed me by about forty pounds, stood head to toe in black, had arms the size of a garage door, and a head the size of a concrete block. His hair was black and oily, and he had a wicked scar on his neck that could only have been caused by a sharp object such as a knife or a grazing bullet. Or maybe he'd encountered Ian's ex-wife.

Steroid-man shoved me onto the stage—without the benefit of an audience—and slapped me around until I started bleeding. I continued to smirk at him, and that's probably why he kept hitting me.

Veronica encouraged the all-out assault, and I drifted in and out of consciousness.

When I came to again, I had metal between my legs, rope wrapped around my entire body, including my neck, the stage about twenty or so feet below me, a grate where I could see the site of my demise, and I had steroid-man peering down at me, two paces away, with a giant grin on his face and not a scratch on him. It just didn't seem right that I had to suffer all of the abuse. And I didn't know how many more lights-out experiences I could take without risking brain damage.

"Nobody will come to help you now," she said. She stood on the stage directly below me, peering up at me with harsh eyes, projecting her voice as if she stood next to me. "You just reached the end of your lives, and my little problem will now go away forever. I knew I couldn't trust Kathryn Gable, she was a bit too unstable for my liking, but she'll come around to my way of thinking once she realizes what is at stake." She might have nodded, the head movement subtle, forced.

"No good deed goes unpunished," I said.

"Your empty threats mean nothing to me. As soon as I give Antoine the go, your problems are no longer my problems. And this time there is nothing that can save you."

And, right on cue, that's when the party started.

A siren materialized in the background.

"You set me up," she said.

I just shrugged, as much as I could with my hands tied behind my back and enough rope wrapped around me to finish the job.

Antoine didn't take it well. He punched me in the gut, and despite my solid abs, his punch felt like more than a bee sting. I struggled to keep my balance. I did, however, bounce a bit, which caused a shot of pain in my testicle region.

The siren became louder. Ian let it rip for all it was worth.

I had a lot of fun watching the party unfold. It's nice to let your opponents think they're the ones running the show, and then you pull the mat right out from under them. As they crash to the floor, and you know you've won, that takes the cake, the ice cream, the whipped cream, and the chocolate sauce.

"Finish him," Veronica ordered. "We can still make it out of here before the cops arrive. I'll let them clean up the mess, and my little problem will be extinct."

Antoine hesitated.

Veronica screamed at him to do it, her face turning three shades of purple. She gestured frantically, wildly, her arms moving as though she conducted a swimming exhibition.

I stared up at my fate-maker: His expression was grim. He shoved me forward on the cat walk.

There was a rush of air, a lurch of the rope, and then I dangled from metal as the grate held me firmly in place, the noose tightening around my neck. I didn't jerk; I didn't squeal; I didn't cough; otherwise, the rope would have cut into my neck even deeper. I estimated I had about forty seconds before my expiration date was up.

Before I started coughing, the door burst open. And if I didn't have my hands tied behind my back, the rope strangling the life out of my throat, and if I hadn't been dangling from the metal staring at the stage below me, with the ceiling much closer than I would have liked, I would have used the powers I'd been given to kick some serious butt. As it was, I couldn't kick any butt, even my own.

"Nobody move," Ian said.

Veronica and Antoine decided this was the perfect time to run. So they did. Metal squealed in protest and jerked me around harder, my body flopping around like a sea bass as Antoine shoved himself away from me, his body banging and lurching with each step. As for Veronica, she exited stage right, her heels clicking on wood, and slammed right into two cops, knocking both of them to the ground. A third one grabbed her around the waist and then shoved her to the ground, right before he slapped on the handcuffs.

Ian looked up, saw me dangling, and then muttered something I couldn't understand. Two cops moved toward the stage while Ian aimed his pistol right at me. Three shots happened in quick succession, I fell in a mad rush to the floor below, the momentum shoving my legs forward as I landed on my back. The wood coughed in protest, or maybe that was me. I didn't try to stand; I waited for Ian to stick out his hand.

He slapped me on the back, shook his head, and told me I needed to stop putting myself in precarious situations. I coughed and sputtered and might have even grimaced.

I told him I'd stop as soon as he decided married life was no longer for him so we could go out on the town, pick up women, and raise a little hell. He didn't laugh; he didn't smirk; his mouth didn't even twitch.

"So did you get all of that?" I asked, removing the wire. At least it had been taped to my front.

"Every word," he said. "There's no way she's going to talk herself out of this one. She may have been sneaky, but we're even sneakier."

"How far do you think he'll get?"

"Not very far," he said. "I have cops all around the building forming a perimeter, and I had three guys already headed for the balcony."

"That's pretty much all you can hope for," I said.

Ian slapped me on the shoulder, and then a series of shouts and much swearing ensued, a punch or two might have been thrown by Antoine before he was tackled to the ground. I peered at Veronica as she squirmed and screamed, and I gave her one of my best grins. If she'd had her hands available, I had the distinct impression she might have given me the finger.

I'd gotten my man, or in this case, woman; I'd wrapped up the case as clean as I could get it; I felt as frisky as I'd ever been; my neck burned; Ian had shown up right on schedule; I didn't have to do the chasing; the wire had served its purpose; two cases were now closed; and my back had its own heartbeat. I had the whole world in front of me, string bikinis included.

I needed another vacation.

Acknowledgments

There's a never-ending cast of characters who made my second novel possible: I'd like to thank Rainbow Books, Inc. for sticking with me one more time; my mom, who always fills my life with encouragement and praise; my dad, who singlehandedly talked me up all over Fairmont to anyone who would listen; Jen, the only one I've found who can keep me on track and on point, even if I don't always listen; my extended family for flooding Amazon with orders and helping me out any way they can (I love all of you!); all the folks who read my unpolished writing; all my readers who give me faith and encouragement every day; and all the folks I've met who provided a source of inspiration. And I'd like to thank God, who always makes the impossible possible. Any errors in judgment have, and always will be, my own.

About the Author

Robert aspired to be a writer before he realized how difficult the writing process was. Fortunately, he'd already fallen in love with the craft, otherwise Casey might never have seen print. Originally from West Virginia, Robert has lived in Virginia, Massachusetts, New Mexico, and now resides in California. *Graceful Immortality* is his second novel. To find out more about Casey, visit the author's website:

www.RobertDowns.net